Praise for Courtney She

the KINDNESS CLUB
Designed by Lucy

"Sheinmel's ability to embody the tween perspective shines in the recklessly energetic Lucy." —*School Library Journal*

"The author allows the complications to build slowly as she develops her title character and demonstrates the ins and outs of fifth-grade friendship." —*Kirkus Reviews*

the KINDNESS CLUB
Chloe on the Bright Side

"Super fun and totally charming! Every kid will want to join the Kindness Club!" —**Sarah Mlynowski**, *New York Times* bestselling author of the Whatever After series

"A great big hug of a book that proves friendships are built one small act of kindness at a time." —**Michael Buckley**, *New York Times* bestselling author of the Sisters Grimm and NERDS series

"A warm and charming first installment."
—*School Library Journal*

"Chloe is a modern-day Pollyanna, spreading kindness everywhere she goes." —*Booklist*

the KINDNESS CLUB
CLUB
Designed by Lucy

COURTNEY SHEINMEL

BLOOMSBURY
CHILDREN'S BOOKS
NEW YORK LONDON OXFORD NEW DELHI SYDNEY

For Susan DeLaurentis, Elizabeth Glaser,
and Susie Zeegen, who started a kindness club of
their own, not so long ago

BLOOMSBURY CHILDREN'S BOOKS
Bloomsbury Publishing Inc., part of Bloomsbury Publishing Plc
1385 Broadway, New York, NY 10018

BLOOMSBURY, BLOOMSBURY CHILDREN'S BOOKS, and the Diana logo are trademarks of
Bloomsbury Publishing Plc

First published in the United States of America in November 2017
by Bloomsbury Children's Books
Paperback edition published in November 2018

Bloomsbury books may be purchased for business or promotional use. For information
on bulk purchases please contact Macmillan Corporate and Premium Sales Department at
specialmarkets@macmillan.com

ISBN 978-1-68119-899-6 (paperback)

The Library of Congress has cataloged the hardcover edition as follows:
Names: Sheinmel, Courtney, author.
Title: Designed by Lucy / by Courtney Sheinmel.
Description: New York : Bloomsbury, 2017. | Series: The Kindness Club ; [2]
Summary: The Kindness Club takes on two new tasks, one, to do a project with children
at the Community House, and two, to plan a surprise birthday party at Tanaka Lanes.
Identifiers: LCCN 2017009977
ISBN 978-1-68119-117-1 (hardcover) • ISBN 978-1-68119-118-8 (e-book)
Subjects: | CYAC: Clubs—Fiction. | Friendship—Fiction. | Kindness—Fiction. |
Schools—Fiction. | Family life—Fiction.
Classification: LCC PZ7.S54124 Des 2017 | DDC [Fic]—dc23
LC record available at https://lccn.loc.gov/2017009977

Book design by Colleen Andrews and Jeanette Levy
Typeset by Westchester Publishing Services
Printed and bound in the U.S.A. by Berryville Graphics Inc., Berryville, Virginia
2 4 6 8 10 9 7 5 3 1

All papers used by Bloomsbury Publishing Plc are natural, recyclable products
made from wood grown in well-managed forests. The manufacturing processes
conform to the environmental regulations of the country of origin.

To find out more about our authors and books visit www.bloomsbury.com
and sign up for our newsletters.

Kindness is always fashionable.
—Amelia Barr

CHAPTER 1

"What page do we have to do in the math workbook?" my friend Chloe asked. "Twenty-five?"

"I'm not sure," I said.

Chloe nudged Theo. He took off his headphones, and she repeated the question: "What's the math homework?"

"Pages twenty-four and twenty-five," Theo replied.

Theo is another friend of mine, and together, we're the three founding members of the Kindness Club. I'd invited them over for an unofficial TKC meeting.

That's how we all became friends, by the way. The Kindness Club. A couple weeks ago, it was a homework project for science. The assignment was to conduct any experiment we wanted. It sounds cool—when a teacher tells you that you can do anything. But really it's incredibly hard, because there are so many possibilities. Almost too many.

After a lot of debate, we decided to test the effect of kind acts on mean people. Would they turn kind, too? There were mixed results. Chloe was kind to the most popular girls in the fifth grade, who also happen to be the meanest girls, and they didn't exactly change their ways. They said Chloe could be their friend, but if and ONLY if she stopped being friends with Theo and me. Chloe told them no, and they were as mean as ever before.

But that was okay, because our experiment worked on another subject—my neighbor, Mary Clare Gallagher. I call her "Mrs. G" for short. She had a disastrous backyard, and a pretty bad front yard, too. Chloe, Theo, and I cleaned it up, and Mrs. G went from being the meanest person I'd ever met to being my friend. That's because when you do something kind for someone, they get a boost of a chemical in their brain called serotonin. It makes them feel good, and sometimes it makes them act kind right back.

It's not that I was a mean person before we started the club, but I wasn't kind as much as I could've been. Unlike Chloe, who always thought up kind things to do. Now I want to be like that, too. After we finished our experiment, we decided to keep the club, and keep up our kindnesses.

So here Chloe and Theo were at my house on a Wednesday. Chloe flipped open the math workbook to the right page. Theo put headphones over his ears and opened his workbook. I felt very happy having them with me in my living room. Even though we were doing homework, which isn't the best activity. Having friends there when you do any activity, good or bad, is so much better than being by yourself.

I used to be by myself a lot. Not by choice. But before Chloe moved to town, and we got assigned the science project together, I didn't have many friends. To be honest, I didn't really have *any*. Some of my classmates thought I was weird because of the outfits I wore.

Okay, I'll admit it. My outfits are different than what other kids at school wear. Their clothes are on the plain side, regular jeans and regular shirts. Or if they're getting dressed up for special occasions, they wear things like you see in a magazine. Which is fine. I'm not making fun of them for copying anything. That's just not for me. I design things myself. I'm practicing for when I grow up and become a fashion designer, just like Diane von Furstenberg and Carolina Herrera and Donatella Versace. Names that when you hear them, you think: *style.*

I'm already a little bit of a fashion designer now. You should see my "Scenes from a T-shirt" collection. They were plain shirts when I bought them, but I painted them. One shirt is a scene from a forest, another is a scene from New York City, and yet another is an underwater fantasyland. I had the best time painting the mermaids and mermen on that one. Every time I finish making an item of clothing, I sew on one of the custom-made tags I ordered off the Internet. They say: "Designed by Lucy."

But anyhoo, even if my clothes are on the original side,

is that a reason to NOT be friends with someone? I don't think so. Luckily, Theo and Chloe don't think so, either.

"You guys," I said. "It's time to call this meeting to order. We have some business to discuss."

"What business?" Chloe asked.

Theo had his headphones on again, and I poked him so he knew to listen up, too. He lifted the left earpiece. "Club business," I said. "We need to make some rules, like how many kind things do we have to do a day?"

"Easy," Chloe said. "As many as we can."

"I think we should set a number," I said. "Something small. Like, three required kind acts a day."

"Okay," Chloe said.

"And when should we have meetings?" I asked.

"How about whenever we want them?"

"Works for me," Theo said.

He was about to lower the left earphone back to his head, but I wasn't done yet. "What about our kindness projects?" I went on. "I think we should do little things all the time, like give compliments, and hold doors open, and drop lucky pennies for people to find. At least three of those a day—and of course you can do more if you want. And we need a big club project to do all together, too."

"Mrs. Gallagher's yard is our big project," Theo said.

"It *was*," I said. "But it's basically all cleaned up now. I know we said we'd plant a garden for her, too. But it's going to be winter soon, and that's more of a spring project.

Meanwhile, what's our next project going to be? We need to figure it out and get started right now."

As long as we had a project, I knew we'd have a club. And if we had a club, I had built-in friends.

But without a project, I was worried the club would disappear. And then maybe Chloe and Theo would decide there wasn't a reason to come over to my house on a Wednesday, or any other day for that matter.

"Sorry," Chloe said. "Right now I have to do my homework. My dad likes me to get as much as possible done before dinner, so he can spend time with me."

Chloe's parents are divorced. That's why she moved to Braywood and started at our school this year. She lives with her mom, except for every other weekend and every Wednesday night, when she is with her dad.

"How about if we do homework *and* think about a club project," I said. "We'll multitask."

"The ability to multitask is really a misconception," Theo informed us. "The human brain can't perform two high-level functions at once. You can do various low-level things all at the same time, like breathing and blinking and pumping blood." He held up a finger and waved it toward me. "But only *one* high-level task at a time."

"Okay, fine," I said. "Homework it is."

Theo re-donned his headphones. Chloe flipped the page in her math book. I opened mine, too. When we finished, we each moved on to reading the chapter in our social studies textbook, though my mind was wandering to thoughts of our club. Maybe I could prove Theo wrong and actually do two "high-level" tasks at the same time—my homework *and* come up with a new kindness project. There's a first time for everything, right?

Hmmm . . . what could our kindness project be?

We could write letters to kids around the world. Though that might be tough, because we didn't speak all of the world's languages.

We could pay the meters for all the cars parked on Main Street. But that would take a lot of quarters—more than we probably had.

We could read to the younger kids in school during story time. Except our teacher, Ms. Danos, probably wouldn't let us out of class for that.

Maybe if I came up with a club motto, the idea for a project would follow. That happens sometimes when I'm designing outfits. I don't know what to make, but then I think of a color or a pattern, and the rest follows.

So . . . a motto . . .

It had to be catchy, and it had to capture exactly what the Kindness Club is all about. I supposed it could just be "Be Kind," but that was so basic, like wearing a plain white T-shirt and jeans. Sure, it counted as being dressed up for the day, but it wasn't exactly inspiring.

But I didn't want our motto to be too complicated, either. Then we'd never remember it.

I thought and thought and thought. It turned out that Theo was right about multitasking. The thoughts of the perfect motto kept me from reading more than a paragraph in my social studies text. But the good news was, by the time Chloe and Theo had to head home, I'd come up with the answer—a perfect motto. In fact, it was more than a motto; it was a full-out cheer. As my friends packed up their bags, I taught it to them:

"I'll say, 'Our brand is,' and you say, 'Kindness!' Ready?"

"Yup."

"Our brand is—"

"Kindness!"

"Our brand is—"

"Kindness!"

"Cool," I said. "That's great, don't you think?"

"I do," Chloe said, "and I'll see you tomorrow."

"See you."

CHAPTER 2

My brother Oliver is away at college, and he left me in charge of feeding his betta fish, Poseidon. Poseidon is five and a half years old, which is old for a betta fish. He's Ollie's prize possession. But since Ollie and I are not only brother and sister but also best friends, he trusts me to take care of him.

I fed Poseidon his dinner, and then I went downstairs to the kitchen to have dinner with Grandma June. She'd set another place for my dad, but he didn't get home from work in time to eat with us.

"This is the fourth night in a row he's missed," I told Grandma as I put tinfoil over his plate. Well, a bowl, really. Inside were rice noodles with beef on top. Keeping it fresh for Dad could count as one of my kind acts for the day. I knew it was one of his favorite meals that Grandma cooked.

My grandmother has lived with my family since my mom died nine years ago. She had a problem with her heart, and the doctors said she'd be okay. But then she got sicker and she died. I was only a year old when it happened, too young to remember anything. All my life that I *can* remember, Grandma June has done the cooking in our house, and that means a lot of Japanese food. Which is fine, since it's mostly stuff I like—except when she makes salmon. That's my least favorite kind of food. Maybe because Poseidon is orange colored, too. I'd never eat him!

"Your dad has to work late, you know that," Grandma June told me.

"Yeah, I know," I said.

Dad owns a bowling alley in our town, and if you're thinking that's the coolest thing a parent could do as a job, you'd be right. At Tanaka Lanes, there are speakers set up so music is pumped into the room from morning till night, and the lanes flash different colors. Sometimes on weekends, Dad makes up a theme, like Disco Fever or Eighties Night, and the whole place is transformed. My favorite was Sock Hop Night. I made my own poodle skirt from a pattern I found online. It was baby pink and shaped like a triangle with a wide bottom. Plus the pièce de résistance: I stitched a little black poodle into the bottom right corner, with its leash curling up into the waistband.

But anyhoo, back to my conversation with Grandma. "It stinks that Felix left before Dad had a chance to hire someone new and train them," I said. Felix had been the manager at Tanaka Lanes until he'd up and quit a week earlier. Dad always used to say Felix was more like his partner than his employee; Dad was the "ideas guy," and Felix was good at carrying things out and keeping it all very organized. "Aren't people supposed to give two weeks' notice?" I asked Grandma.

"How do you know about two weeks' notice?" she said.

"I saw it in a movie."

Grandma opened the fridge to put away the water pitcher. "Well," she said, her back to me as she rearranged the top shelf, "it's your father's name on the sign out front. If someone is unavailable, it's up to him to fill in the missing pieces."

"And you too," I told her.

"What?" She closed the door and turned around to face me.

"And you too," I repeated. "You've been helping Dad out."

"That's what family does."

"Maybe I should, too," I said. "I bet Chloe and Theo would come with me. We need a project for the Kindness Club!"

"That's sweet of you to offer your services to the bowling alley. But for now I think your dad and I have it covered."

"Tell us if you change your mind."

"I certainly will."

I brought my plate to the dishwasher, but Grandma stopped me from opening it. "No, *mago*," she said. That's the Japanese word for "grandchild," which is what Grandma always called Ollie and me, the way other grandparents may say "honey" or "dear." "Just leave it in the sink. I'm going to hand wash everything. The dishwasher broke this morning."

"It broke?" I asked. "How?"

"It got old, that's all," Grandma said. "It's the same dishwasher that was here when I moved in, which makes it older than you are, most likely."

"You always tell me how young I am," I reminded her.

"People and appliances age at different rates," Grandma told me.

"I get it," I said. "Like Poseidon. Five and a half years old for him is like a hundred in human years. Older than you!"

"I'm getting up there," Grandma said.

"No, you're not, and besides, you look great for your age," I said, which was sixty-eight.

I was being nice when I said that, because to be honest, I couldn't tell if she looked good for her age, or average, or even on the old side. But whatever it was, I loved the way she looked. In old pictures, I could tell her hair had once been jet black, but now it was mostly gray and cut to just above her shoulders. She usually had it pinned up very neatly on either side. Her skin was tan and smooth and soft as a peach, except for right around her eyes, where the skin was on the crinkly side, and her elbows, which were *really* crinkly. When I was a little kid and she'd hold me in her lap, I would reach out to play with her elbow crinkles. I can't explain why, but it made me feel cozy.

"You don't look a day over sixty-five," I told her.

Grandma smiled her trademark closed-mouth smile. She doesn't like her teeth so she hardly ever shows them. The right front tooth sticks out a little bit over the left one. It's something that I kind of like about her mouth. It's different, and it makes her mouth just so her. Sometimes she'll forget and smile with her teeth, and seeing it is like discovering a secret.

We stood next to each other at the sink. Grandma turned on the tap to super hot and gave me a pair of rubber gloves to wear so my skin wouldn't burn. I squirted a circle of dish soap onto her dirty dinner plate. It looked a bit like a head, so I added a few dots for two eyes, a nose, and a little open mouth.

"I think you have enough there," Grandma said.

I put down the soap and picked up the scrub brush. "When do you think we'll get a new dishwasher?" I asked.

"Tired of this chore already, I see," Grandma said.

"No, I was just wondering."

"I guess whenever your dad or I have time to go to the store. But it's all right. I'll take it from here. Sometimes washing the dishes relaxes me."

"Are you stressed out?" I asked. "Maybe you shouldn't have so many jobs. You're working at the bowling alley, and you volunteer a lot. You do so much around here. Plus you just took that job at Quinnifer's. I think it's too much!"

"Nonsense," Grandma said. "It's good to keep busy and stay useful."

"But I'm worried about you."

"You don't need to worry about me. What you do need to worry about is your own work. How was piano today?"

"Mrs. Negishi is visiting her nephew," I reminded her, feeling worried all over again. "That's why Chloe and Theo got to come over on a Wednesday."

"But you promised to practice in her absence."

"Yeah, I know. I will. I promise. It's so boring, though. Mrs. Negishi has had me playing the same piece for like a year."

"I'm sure it hasn't been a year," Grandma chided. "But if you're still on the same piece, she must feel you haven't mastered it yet. Keep practicing. Piano is good for concentration and coordination. In the end, you'll learn more than just music."

"Right now I'm learning the facial expressions Mrs. Negishi makes when I hit a wrong note in 'Für Elise.'" I turned to her and tried to imitate them, a scrunched-up nose and turned-down mouth, like I'd tasted something gross.

Grandma smiled—closed mouthed. "And what about your homework?" she asked. "Did you and your friends get that all done?"

"Everything except social studies," I told her. No point in telling her that Chloe and Theo *had* finished. I'd get it done, too. "I have to finish the chapter on westward expansion and answer some questions."

"That sounds interesting."

I shrugged. "Did you learn about the pioneers going west when you were in school?"

She shook her head. "By the time we moved to the States, the teachers had already taught those lessons. But I studied on my own a lot. My parents kept speaking Japanese at home, but as soon as I learned enough English, it was the only language I'd speak. I wouldn't answer to my given name. I went bowling because it seemed like a very American pastime."

"Dad said bowling actually started in ancient Egypt."

"He's right," Grandma said. "But I didn't know that then. My new friends hung out at the bowling alley, and I wanted to be like everyone else."

"Not me," I told her. "I like being unique."

I've never met anyone exactly like me before. People think I'm Japanese, but that's only three-quarters true. My dad is 100 percent Japanese, but my mom was only 50 percent. The other 50 percent was African American. She had dark skin and wavy black hair. There's a photo on my dresser from my first birthday. I'm holding my favorite bear, Timber, in my right hand. My left arm is stretched above my head, my fingers twisted up in my mother's hair. Her name was Leilani, which means "heavenly flowers" in Hawaiian.

My point is, whether it's on the inside, like my genes I got from my parents, or on the outside, like the jeans I made for myself, I'm different from everyone else.

"I know you like your uniqueness, my mago," Grandma said. "It's an excellent quality."

"Thank you," I said, feeling pleased. My grandmother is always nice, but she's also the kind of person who only gives compliments when she means them.

"Now, speaking of history," Grandma said, "you should go on and do your work."

I took off the rubber gloves, handed them to Grandma, and headed up to Oliver's room, which is my favorite space to do my homework. His room is bigger than mine. Mine is the size of a closet—a big closet, but still a closet. In fact, it really *was* once a closet. I had a real bedroom-sized room when I was born, but then Grandma moved in, and they made up the closet room for me. It has a bed in it, and a dresser pushed up against the opposite wall. You can just barely open the drawers all the way. When Ollie left for college, Dad said he should switch rooms with me and stay in the closet when he visited. But I didn't want to change things. My room is still my room. I just use my brother's for homework purposes, and to visit Poseidon.

The chapter I needed to read started on page fifty-two: why the pioneers went west. Basically, they were poor and they wanted to get rich. Their stuff was old and damaged. They mended holes in their clothing and kept wearing it. They didn't have money to worry about how things looked or if they were in fashion. They just patched things together and kept wearing them—shirts, pants, socks, blankets. But they thought they were headed west for a better life. Along the way a lot of people got sick and died. Maybe some of them had weak hearts, like my mom. I bet if the pioneers had known what would happen, most of them would've kept on living right where they were.

I flipped the page and looked at the comparison maps of the United States, then and now. Back then, before westward expansion, there were some states sectioned off in the east, but the west was one big gray area.

All fifty states were in the "now" map, carved out from east to west, colored in different colors. There was no gray area left. It was its own kind of patchwork quilt, like the ones the pioneer women made. Lines were drawn seemingly haphazardly. Idaho really was a funny shape. Our own state of Maryland was so teeny-tiny, while Texas was really big.

I wondered who decided what borders went where. And who decided on the shapes of things? Michigan was shaped like a mitten, which was cool. But none of the other states looked like clothes. If I was designing things, I'd even out the size of things to be fair, and I'd definitely change the shapes. More clothing shapes, like sunglasses for California, and maybe a cowboy hat for Colorado. And I'd add other shapes, too, like flowers and stars, even a horseshoe, or the head of a unicorn.

Down the hall, I heard the phone ring. It was probably Ollie. I flipped my textbook shut and headed out.

CHAPTER 3

The phone rang a second time, then a third, as I walked toward the kitchen. Grandma was probably drying her hands before picking up the receiver. "Hello?" she said as I came through the doorway.

"Hey, Ollie!" I shouted.

Grandma brought a finger to her lips to signal I should be quiet. Not Ollie after all. I was about to slink away when I heard Grandma say, "Shoot," into the phone. That was about as close as my grandmother got to a curse word, and she didn't even use that one very often. "I'm working a part-time job at Quinnifer's . . . yes, that's right, the stationery store. I'm on tomorrow. Since it's only my second shift, I'm afraid I can't ask them to let me out of it. I am so embarrassed about this, Valerie."

The person on the other end of the phone, Valerie,

must've said something back, because Grandma paused and leaned against the counter.

"Mmm hmm," she said. "I know you're understaffed as it is, so that's very understanding of you. Thank you."

"Is everything all right?" I asked after Grandma hung up. She looked at me like she hadn't known I was there, hanging in the doorway, listening to her half of the conversation the whole time.

"Oh, yes," she said. "I just forgot I was signed up to volunteer at the Community House tomorrow."

Ever since I started school full time, back in kindergarten, Grandma has been one of Braywood's premier volunteers. She fund-raises for the library, makes meals for needy families at the food pantry, reads to residents at the senior center every Tuesday, and works at the Community House every Thursday, where she looks after kids whose parents have jobs that keep them out later than the end of the school day.

"But you always volunteer on Thursday afternoons," I reminded her.

"I know," she said. "I guess I've been so busy that I forgot what day it was."

"You forgot what *day* it was?"

"Temporary amnesia," Grandma said.

I hoped it was temporary. I read a book once about a girl whose grandfather had something called Alzheimer's disease, and he forgot more and more things until he forgot almost everything—including his granddaughter's name.

"How did your social studies homework go?" Grandma asked.

Phew. She remembered I was doing my social studies homework. "It was fine," I said. "I didn't do the questions at the back of the chapter yet, but I finished all the reading. You know what Theo told me . . ." I let my voice trail off.

"What? What did Theo say?"

"Oh my goodness."

"What?" Grandma repeated.

"Oh my goodness. Oh my goodness. Oh my goodness! I just had an idea. And it's such a good one." I rubbed my hands together, as if I'd discovered something. "I can't believe I didn't think of it before. This is so perfect."

"Well, don't keep me in suspense."

"We can volunteer for you," I said triumphantly. "The Kindness Club. Call Valerie back and tell her."

"I appreciate this, Lucy. But you don't have to do this—and your friends certainly don't have to. The three of you aren't responsible for my missed obligations. I'm sure they'll manage at the Community House tomorrow. Perhaps they'll put on a movie for the kids. That usually works to keep everyone quiet and contained—at least for a little while."

"Or they can do a super cool project with us," I said. "Come on, you said family helps out."

"I did, but—"

"I really want to do this. I mean *we*. *We* really want to do this. Every club needs a project, and we don't have one right now. What if, well, what if we never get one?"

"You think you'd lose your club?"

"I don't know. I hope not. It's the first time I've really belonged in something—I mean, outside our family, of course."

"The thing is, Lucy," Grandma said. "Some of the kids at the Community House are not much younger than you are. I know how mature and helpful you are—but Valerie may think I'm just handing her three more kids she needs to look out for."

"She won't have to look out for us. We can do this. I know we can."

"I know you can, too."

"So can't you explain it to her," I said. "Please."

Grandma nodded. "Let's give it a shot. Call your friends and see what they think. If they're free, I'll call Valerie."

"Great!" I grabbed the phone from the base and began to dial Theo's number.

"Lucy?" Grandma said. When I looked at her, she was smiling, and a sliver of her teeth showing. "Thank you," she said.

I smiled back. "You're welcome," I told her as Theo picked up on the other end. "Hi," he said.

"Hi back! I just had the best idea for the club! Wait till you hear this!"

CHAPTER 4

Theo said yes about volunteering at the Community House, and then we three-way-called Chloe at her dad's, and she agreed to come, too. Grandma called Valerie back to let her know.

I listened to Grandma explain about the Kindness Club, and I knew Valerie must've said we could come, because Grandma pressed the button to put the call on speakerphone, so I could talk, too.

"Valerie Locklin, meet my granddaughter, Lucy."

"It's so nice to meet you," I said.

"It's very good to meet you, too," she told me. "We'll be happy to have you and your friends help out tomorrow."

She went through the rundown of what Chloe, Theo, and I could expect. Basically there'd be about fifteen kids in the big rec room, ranging in age from really little, like preschool age, to third grade, which was just two years younger than us. But those two years make a big difference. I'm much more mature now than I was when I was eight years old.

"We try to arrange a big project each day for everyone to work on," Valerie Locklin told me. "But we don't have anything like that on the schedule for tomorrow."

"It was my job to come up with something," Grandma broke in. "I'm sorry to say I didn't get a chance to do so."

For a second, that knot of fear in my stomach came back. Another forgotten thing.

"Don't worry about it," Valerie Locklin said. "We don't always have a coordinated project. But if you don't mind, Lucy, I may ask that you and your friends split up. One of you may be helping the grade schoolers with homework. Another may be doing finger painting with the little ones, and a third might be reading to kids in the story corner. We ask that our volunteers be flexible. That sound okay to you?"

"Oh, yes," I said. "Flexible is my middle name—and it's Chloe's and Theo's, too."

Of course Valerie Locklin knew I was kidding, and she laughed. "Good to hear," she said. "I'll plan on seeing the three of you tomorrow."

I have a lot of thoughts at night when everyone else I know is sleeping, and I'm supposed to be sleeping, too. It's not that I don't want to be sleeping. In fact, I try to sleep; I really do. I close my eyes and attempt to hypnotize myself into a not-awake state: *You are getting very sleepy, Lucy Melia Tanaka. That's right. Very verrrrrrrrrrrry sleepy. Now go to sleep, Lucy. Go to SLEEP SLEEP SLEEP!*

It doesn't always work, because other thoughts kick in, such as: *What will I wear to school tomorrow? And the day after that? And after that?*

Sometimes when I finally fall asleep, the answers to my fashion questions come in my dreams. That night I was thinking about what to wear to the Community House. Something that said, *Hey, kids, I'm a totally fun person to hang out with.* It had to be that, plus something I wouldn't care about if the kids accidentally smudged it with un-wash-off-able finger paint. That was a problem, because I cared about most of my clothes.

I rolled over in my bed, burrowing into the corner, the coziest spot. I squeezed my eyes shut and tried to focus on dreaming up the perfect outfit. But other things were pinging around my brain. Thoughts of Grandma being forgetful. It wasn't like her at all. Usually she remembered EVERYTHING. She remembered whether the dishes in the dishwasher were clean or dirty without having to open it and check (back when our dishwasher still worked). She remembered when I had spelling quizzes and math tests and every other school thing, and she made sure I studied enough. She remembered things for my dad and my brother, too. It was like her brain was some kind of safe deposit box.

But what if it cracked open? What if she forgot my study schedule, and whether the dishes had been cleaned, and whatever Dad and Ollie needed her to remember? What if she forgot *me*, like the grandfather in that book?

This isn't a book, Lucy, I told myself silently but sternly. *There's nothing to worry about, so think about something different. If clothing isn't working, then you should think about . . . hmm . . . think about sheep! Yes, that's it. That's what you should think about. Counting them is supposed to make you sleepy, even though that sounds pretty silly. But don't knock it till you've tried it.*

Okay, here it goes: One invisible sheep, jumping over the bed. It's white and fluffy, like a robe . . . with a face and a few limbs. Okay, that's weird, but you need to keep going, Lucy, because you're not sleeping yet. Two sheep. Three, four.

Ugh.

It wasn't working. I was still awake. Possibly even wider awake than I was before I started imagining sheep leaping above me. Thoughts are like bowling balls. You always want them to go one way, straight down the center of the lane, and knock down all the pins you're aiming for. But a lot of the time they veer off course. Sometimes so far off course that you don't get any pins down at all.

I hit the light switch beside my bed, because I don't like sitting in the dark for too long. It's not that I'm scared of it. It just feels lonely. With the lights on, I was still alone, but I could see my "fashion wall," where I tack up things I've ripped out from magazines, and my dresser with the framed pictures on top, and the end of my bed with my stuffed animals. Some kids think ten is too old to keep stuffed animals on your bed, but I am not one of those kids. I looked at the row of them—Pammy, Patty, Monku, Furry, and Timber.

Of course Timber. I reached down to the end of my bed and picked him up. He looked much better in the picture of Mom and me. Since then, his pink nose had been rubbed white, and one of his ears was gone. I sat him right next to me and put a hand on his head, thinking about my mom. I didn't remember her, except for things I saw in pictures. I thought I could remember that day, my first birthday, sitting in her lap with brand-new Timber. I played that moment in my head over and over again, like a movie on repeat in my brain.

Did Mom name Timber for me? Or did I come up with the name myself? That part I couldn't remember at all. That part wasn't in the memory-movie.

There was a soft knock on the door, and then someone pushed it open. "Lucy?"

"Hi, Dad."

He stood in the doorway wearing pajama bottoms and one of his work shirts, which was turquoise with a black collar and black buttons. His first name, Kenji, was stitched in black thread over the breast pocket. If he turned around, I knew the back of his shirt would say Tanaka Lanes in bold black letters.

"I saw the light coming from under the door," Dad said. "I thought perhaps you fell asleep with it on."

I shook my head. "Nope. I just haven't fallen asleep yet."

"You shouldn't be up so late, Lucy."

Tell me about it, I thought.

"I wasn't on purpose," I told him. "Did I wake you?"

"No, no," Dad said. "I only got home a few minutes ago."

"Wow, it's really late."

"Work is late sometimes," Dad said with a shrug.

"I told Grandma I could help out, if you need it," I said.

"Tanaka Lanes is my job to take care of," Dad said. "And school is yours. Speaking of which, is your homework done?"

His voice had turned stern, the same tone as when he'd said, *You shouldn't be up so late, Lucy*, and I didn't think I deserved that tone at all. My whole life, I'd always done my homework on time.

Which is exactly what I said to him: "I *always* do my homework on time."

"Just checking," Dad said, back in his regular voice. "Learning anything interesting?"

"Just the usual school sort of stuff," I said. "We're doing a section on the pioneers moving west before there were states out there. But tomorrow—" I cut myself off, as the spark of an idea hit me.

"But tomorrow what?" Dad asked.

"Oh my goodness!" I said, not answering the question.

"What's going on?"

"I just had the best idea. THE BEST!"

"Shush, Lucy, you'll wake Grandma. If you get much louder, you'll wake Mrs. Gallagher, too."

"Sorry," I said in a lower voice. "But I'm helping Grandma out tomorrow. That's what I was about to say. The Kindness Club will be volunteering at the Community House, because that's what Grandma usually does on Thursdays, except she took a shift at the stationery store tomorrow."

"Your poor grandmother," Dad said. "She's spread a little thin these days."

"That's why I said I could help out, too."

He shook his head. "Tell me your idea."

"Valerie Locklin from the Community House said they try to think of a big project all the kids work on together, and I just thought of something to do—we'll make a patchwork quilt! Just like the United States!"

"Shh, Lucy," Dad said. He paused. "What about the United States?"

I lowered my voice again and explained. "If you look at a map, the states all fit together like patches. We could give each of the kids a patch of fabric to decorate. When they're all done, I'll sew all the patches together to make one big Community House quilt. What do you think?"

"I think it's a great idea, and I also think it's time for you to go to sleep."

I pushed my legs back under the covers, but I didn't lie down. I was loving my idea and thinking out loud. "I've got puff paints and fabric markers in practically every color," I said. "But I don't think I have enough fabric, so I'll need to go to Fabric World, or maybe Second Chance."

Second Chance was the thrift store in town, which is a kind of store that sells secondhand things. I know some people don't like buying clothes that used to belong to other people, but it makes them much cheaper and you never know what you'll find. Sometimes I buy things and turn them into other things. Like I could buy a lightweight blanket, cut it up, and turn it into a patchwork quilt.

"Can you loan me some money for the fabric?" I asked Dad. "You owe me a lot of back allowance anyway."

Technically I was supposed to get allowance every Sunday. Ten dollars for being ten years old. But Dad wasn't always great about remembering to give it to me, and he hadn't ever upped it from nine to ten since my birthday.

"Well," he started.

"It shouldn't even count as my allowance," I said. "It's more like you making your own donation to the Community House. It's a great cause. Just ask Grandma."

"I know it's a good cause, Lucy," Dad said. "I'll give you some money in the morning."

"Thank you," I said. "That's so cool of you."

"That's me, Cool Dad," he said. "And now it really is time for my cool daughter to go to sleep. I bet you'll have a better chance of doing so if you actually turn the lights out."

The light in my room is controlled by two switches—the

one by the bed and the one by the door. Dad flipped the switch by the door right then, and the room fell to darkness. I finally lay back down.

"Good night, Goose," Dad said, using an old nickname. Every family has nicknames, I think. Chloe's parents call her "Chloe-bear." I don't know what Theo's parents call him, but I bet he has a special nickname, too. My family calls me "Goose," and "Lucy-Goosey," and a variety of other Lucy-rhyming things. It makes me feel safe. Snug as a bug in a rug.

"Good night," I said.

He shut the door behind him, and just like that the bowling game of thoughts was over, and I was able to fall asleep.

CHAPTER 5

My dream-plan worked, because I woke up with the perfect outfit in mind: my splotchy overalls. They hadn't come splotched. I'd found them at Second Chance and splotched them with bleach myself. If kids at the Community House accidentally spilled paint on my lap, it'd look like I'd planned it that way.

I pulled my hair back in a ponytail and fastened it with a unicorn clip. I was going to use my clown one, but then thought better of it; sometimes kids are afraid of clowns. But I'd never heard of a kid being afraid of unicorns.

After school, Chloe, Theo, and I headed over to the Community House, with a brief stop-off at Theo's. The stop-off was because Dad had left for the bowling alley before I'd even woken up, and he'd forgotten to leave money for me. I asked Grandma, but she didn't have any cash on her, and there wasn't time for her to get any before school.

"Maybe you can improvise," she suggested.

As a budding fashion designer, I'm used to improvising. Not enough black buttons for a shirt, alternate button colors. Outgrow my favorite skirt, add a strip of denim to create more room in the waist. But I couldn't imagine what could possibly take the place of fabric on a quilt. That would be like trying to make a habitat for Poseidon without using any water. Poseidon is a fish! Water is the most essential ingredient!

"You could make a paper quilt," Grandma told me. "There's plenty of paper already at the Community House. Each kid could decorate a square."

"A rectangle," I corrected. "Pieces of paper are usually rectangles."

"Fine, then," she said. "Rectangles will work just as well. You, Chloe, and Theo could collect them and piece them together."

"You can't sew paper."

"So use tape," Grandma said. "Remember this is about improvising. You're a creative girl. This should be second nature to you."

I shrugged. She was right about my creativity, of course. Aside from my uniqueness, it was the quality that usually made me proudest of myself. Still, it's hard to get excited about a paper quilt when you've been envisioning a real one.

"Or you don't have to make a quilt at all," Grandma went on. "Valerie will be happy with your assistance if you simply go over and read to the kids. She isn't expecting any more from you."

"Yeah, I know," I said. I felt a little bit better, but not really. I always like exceeding people's expectations. Besides, when you have a good idea, the thing you want to do is put it into action.

It was time to leave for school, so I kissed Grandma good-bye. My house is smack in the middle of Theo's way to Braywood Intermediate. Not long after we started the club, we began walking to school together. We never talked about it; one day I just happened to walk outside a couple minutes earlier than usual, and there was Theo, passing by. When he saw me he paused to wait. I skipped down the porch steps to the sidewalk and we continued on together.

Every day since, I've tried to time it so I step outside at just about the time he'll be there. If I'm running late, he walks to the front door and knocks twice, a signal to hurry up. But I walked out of the house that day to no Theo. He had an ophthalmologist appointment. His mom would be driving him to school an hour late. I headed down the porch steps, feeling bummed out, partly because I was alone again, but mostly because the puff paints and fabric markers were bulking up my backpack, and we wouldn't get to use them.

At lunch, I filled Chloe and Theo in on the problem: great idea, missing materials. "I'd say we could use my money for fabric," Chloe said. "But I'm still paying my mom back for the ingredients she bought so I could make gluten-free cookies for Sage."

Sage was the daughter of Chloe's dad's new girlfriend, Gloria. At first, Chloe hadn't liked either of them, because she wanted her family back to the way it was before. But she started doing kind things for them, and the serotonin boost in her brain was making things easier.

I turned to Theo. "Don't worry," I told him. "I'm not expecting you to jump in and pay for my idea. That wouldn't be right."

"Being kind doesn't always come with a financial commitment, but sometimes it does," Theo said. "In this case, however, I think I have a more economical solution."

Theo often spoke as if he were forty instead of ten.

"What?" Chloe and I asked at the same time. I was going to say "jinx," but I really wanted to hear Theo's answer.

"My sister kicked a hole in one of her bedsheets overnight."

"Does Anabelle do karate in her sleep?" Chloe asked.

"My dad thinks she must've been having a dream about a track meet and she ran straight through the sheet," Theo said. "But my point is—she tore it, so she isn't going to use it anymore."

My mind flashed to the pioneers, with their patched clothing and blankets. No way they'd trash a sheet just because it had a hole. That sheet may have been the only thing they had to cover themselves at night. But I understood what

Theo was saying. "You mean we could use the sheet at the Community House," I said.

He nodded. "Exactly. It already has one tear, so we'll tear it more. Into as many pieces as we need for all the kids."

"I think we should use scissors so it's neater," Chloe said.

"I was being figurative when I said 'tear,'" Theo said. "I assumed we'd use scissors."

"And after the kids decorate them, I'll stitch the pieces back together to make a quilt!" I exclaimed.

I was so happy to be able to put my plan into effect after all that I threw my apple up in the air and caught it. For a split second my eyes locked with Monroe Reeser's. She was sitting at her usual table at the back of the cafeteria, along with her two best friends, Anjali Sheth and Rachael Padilla. The popular/mean girls. The ones who didn't change, despite the fact that Chloe was awfully kind to them.

As soon as Monroe caught me looking, she looked away and started gabbing to the other girls. The It Girls. That's the name of their club. If our brand is kindness, then their brand is coolness. They're really exclusive about who is cool enough to be in their club. That's fine, I suppose; you don't have to be friends with anyone you don't want to be friends with. But they also make fun of the kids they don't let in, and if you ask me, there's nothing fine about that.

I know Monroe and the others talk about me, and I try not to let it bother me. My brother Oliver would say, "Don't give them the satisfaction." The problem is that when there's a kid like Monroe in your class who's being mean, you can't ignore her completely, because everyone else is listening to what she has to say. So it does matter, and I'm sorry if that gives her satisfaction, but that's the truth.

But enough about Monroe and the It Girls. This moment was about the Kindness Club. "That's great," I told Theo. "Thank you."

"Thank my sister's violent night of sleep."

I looked across the cafeteria, in the direction opposite of Monroe and her friends. Anabelle's a year younger than we are, in fourth grade. I didn't see her, but I still sent her a silent thank-you in my head. In a way, she had done a kind thing. I'd forgotten to count my own kind deeds of the day, but I bet I'd have lots at the Community House now—way more than three.

"Are you sure your mom will still have the sheet?" Chloe asked Theo. "She wouldn't have thrown it away?"

"Nah," he said. "She was going to wash it and bring it over to the office."

Theo's parents have the second coolest jobs in Braywood, right after my dad. And okay, fine: maybe they have the coolest jobs, or at least it's a tie. His father is a veterinarian, and his mother runs an animal rescue clinic. Anabelle sometimes helps them out, but unfortunately for Theo, he's allergic to animals so he can't. He doesn't seem to mind, though. He mostly spends his time reading textbooks that are WAY above our grade level, and trying to make new discoveries. Oh, and doing things for our club, of course.

"It's such a coincidence that we need fabric and you just happen to have some," I said. "What were the chances of that?"

"From a statistical perspective, the probability of coincidence is quite high," Theo said. "A prime example is the so-called 'birthday problem.' If you have twenty-three people in the room, the chance of two of them having the same birthday is fifty percent, even though you wouldn't necessarily think so, with there being three hundred and sixty-five days in a year—or three hundred and sixty-six if it's a leap year. Some people disagree with the conclusions, though."

See what I mean about the kinds of textbooks that Theo reads?

Chloe gently knocked him in the side. "Oh, you," she said.

"What?" he asked.

"I love all the things I learn from you, that's all," she said. "It's like taking another class. I take math, and science, and Spanish, and also Theo."

Theo blushed, but I could tell he was pleased. "You guys will have to be the ones to go in and get the sheet from my mom," he said. "I can't get too close to the clinic. You know, my allergies."

"We don't mind at all," Chloe said.

"It's the opposite of minding," I said. "We actually like going in to see all the animals."

Across the table, Chloe was giving me a funny look, and suddenly I realized what she was thinking: don't rub it in to Theo that he doesn't get to see the animals, too. That's what I mean about Chloe being kind all the time. It seems like she doesn't even try; she's just automatically kind. I mean to be that way, but sometimes I say something before I've thought too hard about it.

But when you know better, you do better. That's what my grandmother says. "We won't have much time with them," I added, so Theo wouldn't feel bad. "I doubt we'll get to pet any of them."

By then lunch was nearly over. We cleaned up our stuff and headed back to Ms. Danos's classroom. The rest of the school day couldn't pass quickly enough. Finally, the last bell rang, and the three of us booked it over to Theo's.

One more coincidence was that the Barnes family lived on Ralston Road, which is almost exactly on the way to the Community House. We could hear dogs barking as we approached. Theo stopped short at the end of the driveway and stood by the mailbox, while Chloe and I ran up the driveway.

Dr. and Mrs. Barnes's office is attached to the house, but it has a separate door, and bells jangled as we pushed it open. The waiting room was filled with about a half-dozen adorable furry creatures (plus one bird), and the humans who'd brought them in. Chloe and I looked out of place, two people and no animals. We told the receptionist who we were, and she called for Mrs. Barnes to come up front. Five minutes later, we were headed back down the driveway toward Theo, bedsheets in hand—the ripped one, plus the matching bottom sheet and pillowcases. That was another thing the pioneers never would've done—give away the matching pieces just because one was ruined. But it was our good luck. I'd use the extra fabric as backing for the quilt.

Mrs. Barnes had washed everything. Chloe balled it all up. We went out to Theo, and on to the Community House.

CHAPTER 6

Valerie Locklin came to the lobby of the Community House to greet us. She was a tall woman with a broad smile. Her dark hair was styled in about a half-dozen uneven braids, each tied with a different-colored ribbon. It was an *interesting* look; not that I was judging or anything. I've been known for sporting some interesting looks of my own.

She held her hand out to shake each of ours—Theo's, Chloe's, then mine.

Back when Oliver was going on his college interviews, he told me it was important for him to look people in the eye and have a firm handshake. It was the first impression the interviewers would have of him. He'd read about it in one of his applying-to-college books. The best handshakes were strong, but not too strong as to break the other person's fingers. You had to strike a balance between not bone-crushing and not weak. If you mastered the perfect handshake, Ollie said, you'd inspire confidence and trust from the other person, and maybe, just maybe, get into your first-choice school.

We practiced together, even though my own college interviews were nearly a decade away. But it came in handy with Valerie Locklin. (Ooh, *hand*-y, get it?!)

"Wow, impressive handshake," she said as she released my hand. "Welcome to the Community Salon."

"Did you just say 'salon'?" Theo asked.

"I did indeed. A few of our premier hairstylists worked me over while we were waiting for you." Ah. That explained all the braids. "They're very excited to have a few big kids visiting today."

"We're so happy to be here, Ms. Locklin," I said. She'd started walking down a brightly lit corridor, and the three of us followed. The carpeting was orange, the walls were yellow, and as we walked, I silently read the signs that had been hung up: "Chess Club Every Monday Night!" "You're Invited to the Senior Mixer!" "Third Annual Talent Show THIS FRIDAY!" "Fundraiser: Let's Bring Racquetball to Braywood!"

"Oh, please, call me Valerie," she said. "We're going to be part of the same team. You can certainly use my first name."

I had been using her first name, in my head. But it was nice of her to tell us to do so out loud. It made me feel older, like she was taking the Kindness Club seriously. I wondered if my handshake had helped.

We'd reached a pair of double doors. Valerie had a hand out to push one open. "Ready?" she said.

"Almost," I said. "There's just one thing I wanted to tell you. I know my grandmother didn't have time to come up with a group project, but we did."

"Well, Lucy did," Chloe broke in. "Theo and I can't take credit."

"We're the Kindness Club," I said. "The ideas of one are the ideas of us all—which is one of the best parts of having a club. And besides, Theo provided the most important material. See the sheets that Chloe's holding?" Valerie nodded. "I brought paint and fabric markers. We thought we could cut the sheet up into pieces, and the kids could each decorate a square. Then I'll bring them home and sew them back together to make a patchwork quilt. What do you think?"

Valerie smiled her broad smile. "I think it's brilliant," she told us. "The kids will absolutely love it." And with that, she pushed open the door into a large, L-shaped room, decorated in bright colors—even brighter than the orange and yellow out in the hall. The bigger part of the L had a long wooden table, which would be the perfect place for the kids to decorate their fabric patches. There were also shelves of books and board games, a couple yoga mats unrolled on the floor, an easel, a bunch of big foam blocks that were stacked almost all the way up to the ceiling, and one of those red-and-yellow plastic cars that little kids can sit in and move around with their feet. The smaller part of the L was a cozy corner with a dark blue throw rug and a couple beanbag chairs.

There were—I counted quickly—twelve kids doing various things. Two kids who looked about six or seven years old were sitting on the beanbag chairs; a much smaller kid was in the car, rolling around and narrowly missing rolling over another little kid's feet. The others were scattered around, at the table, on the floor, in the middle of various games and projects.

Valerie signaled to the other adult in the room to come over and meet us. Her name was Leesha Fox, and she gave us each a hug like we'd known one another for a while, and thanked us for coming in.

A girl who looked to be about five years old, wearing a light pink sweater, pulled on Leesha's hand. "Leesha! Leesha! Who are you talking to?" she asked.

"These are my new friends," Leesha said. "And I think they'll be your friends, too, Hazel."

"Really?" Hazel asked.

"Really."

"I'm about to tell everyone all about them," Valerie added. She clapped her hands, and all around the room, the kids stopped what they were doing and turned their attention to her. Even the kid in the plastic car stopped making his *vroom vroom* noises. He pretended to pull into a parking spot, and looked up at her.

"That's great listening, kids," she said. "And I'm glad to have your attention, because I have three very special friends to introduce you to. This is Lucy, Chloe, and Theo. They are in *fifth grade* at the Braywood Intermediate School."

She said the words "fifth grade" like she was saying we were in college, and the way the kids looked at us, I could tell they were really impressed. It felt like a big deal, even though I know from Ollie that being in college is much more impressive.

"They are in a club called the Kindness Club."

"Ooh," one of the kids said.

"They are surely living up to their name right now," Valerie went on, "because they have a lot of things they could be doing this afternoon, but they decided to come visit us. Let's do our best to make them feel welcome."

"You're welcome here!" a boy in a Baltimore Orioles T-shirt and matching hat called out.

"Good job being welcoming, Damien," Leesha said.

So then all the other kids shouted out: "Welcome!" "Welcome" "Welcome!"

Chloe, Theo, and I all said thanks, and how happy we were to be there. Then Valerie went on. "Not only are they here to play with us today, but also they brought along a special project. Do you guys want to hear about it?"

"Yes!" the kids chorused.

Valerie turned to the three of us, plus Leesha. "Sorry," she said. "It doesn't sound like they want to hear about it."

"No!" the kids screamed. "We do! We do!"

Valerie cupped a hand around her right ear. "What was that? You *do* want to hear about the project?"

"YES!" they screamed, so loudly that the room shook. I was sure everyone else in the building heard, too. Chloe, Theo, and I smiled at one another.

"Okay," Valerie told me. "I guess they want to hear after all, so take it away."

The kids were all looking up at the members of the Kindness Club expectantly, like we were sort of celebrities. I explained the idea, and when I finished, everyone started talking at once. Valerie clapped again and instructed the kids to go to the art corner and get protective aprons to wear. In the meantime, Leesha lined the big table with old news-paper, and Chloe, Theo, and I got busy cutting up the ripped sheet into pieces.

"Can I have that piece?" a girl asked as I snipped off something that looked like a rhombus.

"Sure," I said.

"Can I sit next to you?" asked another.

"I'd like that," I told her.

"No, I want you to sit next to me!" the boy named Damien cried.

"She has *two* sides," the girl informed him. "I'm going to sit with her on my left side, and Chloe on my right."

"And I'm going to sit next to Chloe, too," the first girl said. "She'll be on my left, and Theo can be on my right."

"That's not fair for some people to sit next to two big kids, and others to not have any big kids at all," Hazel said.

"Just sit where you sit, and the big kids, along with Leesha and I, will come around to help," Valerie told everyone.

By then we had Anabelle's old sheet all cut up. I did my best to make some interesting shapes, though it was hard with the kids bouncing up and down all around us. They seemed pleased, though, and each claimed pieces. I pulled my fabric markers and paints out of my backpack. The kids settled around the table, all but one. A girl who I would guess was in first or second grade, wearing black leggings and a white shirt with a kitten decal ironed on it. "Come sit with the group, Frances," Leesha told her.

Frances took a step forward and then stopped. "What if I don't want to decorate a piece for the quilt? Do I still have to sit there?"

"No, of course you don't have to," Leesha said. "But don't you want to? Valerie and I will hang it on the back wall, so everyone who visits will always get to enjoy it."

"No, thank you," Frances said, polite but firm. "I just want to read by myself."

She wandered over to the corner with the throw rug and settled into a beanbag chair with a book.

I felt a little sad that she didn't like my idea, but there were eleven other kids to help. We tied aprons, rolled up sleeves, uncapped markers, and got to work. Chloe, Theo, and

I, plus Valerie and Leesha, walked around the table oohing and aahing at the works in progress.

"They're so adorable," Chloe told me as we stood back and looked on. "I love that we're here doing this."

"Yeah, but—" I lowered my voice. "I wish Frances liked my idea, too. I wanted a project that was good enough for everyone to enjoy."

"Eleven out of twelve kids *did* like your idea," Chloe said. "Look how much fun they're having."

I looked. All the kids except Frances were seated around the table, making a big mess, which I knew meant they were having fun.

"This is a good-enough project," Chloe went on. "More than good enough. It's a great one."

"Hey, you," the little kid from the plastic car called. "Dark-haired girl. I can't remember your name, but I need help!"

I gave Chloe a smile. "Thanks for saying all that," I told her. "Gotta go. Duty calls."

The little boy, whose name turned out to be Wendell, was making an iguana with green puff paint. I thought it was a pretty grown-up-sounding name for a little kid; but I guess all grown-ups were kids once, and his name would fit him just fine when he got older.

Wendell gave me a handful of smudged fabric markers and began dictating instructions: "Put in green. No, not there, THERE. Now make black eyes. No, his eyes are bigger than that. Yeah, like that. Don't forget that he's got scales on his back."

I didn't even notice that Chloe had wandered away from the table until she came back a few minutes later, Frances's hand in hers. "Lucy," she said. "Can we speak to you for a second?"

"Sure." I turned to Wendell. "Is it okay if I leave you for a minute?"

"Oh, yes," he said. "This lizard is going to breathe fire, and I want to draw the fire by myself."

I patted his shoulder and stepped a couple feet away from the table. Frances was holding tight to Chloe, and I bent down to her level. "Hey," I said in my softest voice. "Are you coming to decorate a patch?"

Frances shook her head and clutched Chloe tighter.

"My new friend Frances was just telling me she doesn't think she's a good artist. I told her that I'm not, either. We were hoping you could help."

"Oh, of course," I said. "I was just helping Wendell, like you saw. Come sit."

I motioned toward the table. Frances dropped Chloe's hand, but she didn't budge. "Wendell is a little kid," she said. "That's why he needs help. I'm big. Not as big as you guys, but I'm bigger than he is, and I want to draw my cat, Nugget."

"That's a great idea," I said. "We don't have any cat patches yet."

"In my head I can picture Nugget like a photograph," Frances said. "She's tan all over, except for her green eyes and pink nose. And she has a tiny white spot on her right front paw. I've tried drawing her before, but it never comes out looking anything like her."

"I understand how you feel," Chloe said. "Whenever I draw anything, it doesn't come out the way it looks in my head. But I can still have fun with it."

"I'm sure you're a better drawer than I am," Frances told her. "I'm sure it's closer to real life when you do it."

"I don't know about that," Chloe said.

"Everything okay over here?" Valerie asked.

"We were just talking about drawing," Chloe said. "How sometimes it doesn't come out the way it looks in your head."

"It NEVER comes out that way for me," Frances said. "I don't want to make a patch. I'm no good at art things."

"That's okay," Chloe said. "I'll still be your friend."

"We all will be," Valerie told her. "But before you decide for sure, can I tell you a secret?"

Frances gave a tiny nod.

"I'm a poet," Valerie said. "There have been plenty of times when I've liked my poems better in my head than on the page. But I keep writing more anyway, and here's why— when I write a poem, I'm creating something that wasn't there before. And that's the cool thing about your patch, if you decide to make one. It'll be something *you* made, your idea and your hard work. Everyone who looks at the quilt will know that part of it wouldn't be there if you hadn't been there to make it."

"It's true," I said. "That's why I design my own clothes. I like making new things."

Chloe smiled at me. "What do you think?" she asked Frances.

"I want to make a Nugget patch," Frances said. "But now it's too late. Everyone else is almost finished."

"I'll sit with you for as long as it takes," Chloe said.

"Me too," I said. "And I can't wait to see it."

Frances nodded okay and took the seat next to Damien, who had drawn a patch for his favorite sports team. He'd covered his piece of the sheet in orange puff paint, and outlined a bird in the middle. He kept touching the middle to see if it had dried yet.

"You have to give it a bit longer," Theo told him. "You have a lot of paint there. The process of evaporation has its work cut out for it. But I have a trick. We can put your patch on the windowsill. The sun will warm it up, and speed up the evaporation process."

"Cool!" Damien said, moving to grab his patch.

"Careful, you better let me do it," Theo said. "You don't want it to smudge. And we should probably put some newspaper down first."

All the kids wanted to move their patches to the sun, and luckily Leesha had plenty of extra newspaper. Frances was bent over her patch on the table, outlining the shape of Nugget with a brown fabric market. Chloe stayed with her, while the grown-ups, Theo, and I carefully carried the finished patches over to the window.

Watching paint dry is boring, even if you have sunlight to speed it up, so Valerie suggested we read while we waited. A girl named Willow pulled a book off the shelf and handed it to me. "This is my favorite. Let's read a chapter of this."

The kids sat around in a circle, and I began to read. After a few minutes, Chloe and Frances were done and came over to join the rest of us. I finished the first chapter, and went on to the second. I was in the middle of the third when parents started showing up. Two and a half hours had gone by since we'd shown up at the Community House. Time had passed quickly, not like we'd been watching paint drying at all.

"Will you be back?" Frances asked Chloe as her mother ushered her to the door.

"You are all welcome to come back and visit anytime," Leesha told us.

"Of course we will be," I said. "We're going to sew the patches together and bring you a finished quilt next week."

"You see, we'll definitely be back," Chloe said.

Frances broke away from her mom to give Chloe a big

hug. Then she hugged Theo and me, too. Most of the other kids were gone at that point. Valerie thanked us again and said we should feel free to leave, too.

"I'm just going to stop in the bathroom before we go," I said. "Can you tell me where it is?"

"Oh, yes, of course," Valerie said. "Go down the main stairwell, take two rights and a left. It's a little tricky. We always accompany the kids. Would you like me to take you?"

"No, thanks, I'm sure I'll find it," I said. "Be right back," I told Chloe and Theo.

CHAPTER 7

The problem wasn't finding the bathroom. The problem was finding my way back to the stairwell when I was done. It was like a maze down there. I couldn't remember the order of the turns, and since it was the end of the day, there weren't any other people. I made a few lefts and a few rights. Nothing looked familiar, so I doubled back and made a right, and then another, hoping for the best. But all I found was another completely different hallway.

How big could the basement of the Community House possibly be?

I stopped for a couple seconds to regroup. I needed a new tactic. Since every turn I thought I should make ended up being wrong, maybe I should do the opposite. I could turn left when I thought I should go right, and perhaps that would finally lead me to the stairwell. And if that didn't

work, well, I guess I'd sleep down here and wait for someone to find me in the morning.

Unless no one ever did find me. I wouldn't have any access
to food or drinks. At this point I didn't even know how to
get back to the bathroom, so I couldn't even use the faucet. I
may as well have been lost in the wilderness. My heartbeat
picked up its pace. No food plus no water equaled Certain
Death.

Calm down, Lucy, I told myself. *Chloe and Theo would
never let you stay lost in the basement forever. They'd send
a search party to find you—or at least they'd send Valerie
and Leesha.*

I walked to the end of the hall to make a left—no, a right.
No, a left. And it was a good choice, because I heard voices.
Civilization, up ahead! I was saved!

I made another left, toward the voices, and walked into
the open doorway of a smallish room. There were six
people there, sitting in chairs arranged in a small circle.
Five of them were kids; but not little kids, like upstairs with
Valerie and Leesha. These kids looked about my age, and
even older. The lone grown-up was a man in black pants
and a navy button-down shirt.

Navy and black together is not my favorite combination.
But you can't tell someone you don't like their fashion choices,
because they may not take it kindly. I've learned that lesson
the hard way. All I can do is keep practicing my designs, and

one day have a line of clothes that I hope everyone buys, because I think they'll look good on everyone!

Someone in the circle sniffled loudly, and someone else passed a box of tissues. "Go on," the man said.

"Odessa said it was because it was too hard for my dad to see it all there hanging in the closet," a girl said. "Like she was just in the other room and she'd be back any minute, looking for her pink silk blouse, or her scarf with the elephants on it. I told my aunt she should've given everything to me. I could've put everything in *my* closet. But she said my closet is too full as it is, and besides that, she said it wouldn't be healthy."

"Maybe you can keep a couple things," an older boy told her. "That's what we did."

"No," the girl said. "Odessa already brought it all to the thrift store. She said it's time to move on, and go back to school, but I really don't want to. I don't want to go back and do things I used to do, like nothing happened." She blew her nose into a tissue. "That's all I want to say."

"Thank you for sharing that," the man said. "Does anyone have something to add?"

"Yeah," a boy said. "There's someone here."

He pointed to the doorway—to me—and the whole circle of people turned to look, including the girl who'd just been talking. I recognized her face as soon as I saw her. It was Serena. Serena Kappas. She was in my grade at school. We'd never been in the same class, even though we'd been going to school together since kindergarten. It seemed improbable that we'd never gotten the same teacher. Like the opposite of Theo's so-called birthday problem.

But still, I did know Serena a little bit. I'd sat with her at lunch a few times, before Chloe moved to town, and she, Theo, and I all became friends. Serena and her best friend Vanessa Medina always had an extra seat at their table. It's not like they were close friends of mine or anything, but they didn't mind when I joined them. At least they never said so.

I raised my hand to wave at Serena. Maybe it was a weird thing to do, since she'd been crying. But what else are you supposed to do when you see someone you've sort of known for half of your life? It was weird to wave, but it would've been weirder not to. Serena gave me the tiniest of tiny waves back.

"May I help you with something?" the man asked me.

I shook my head, but then remembered I *did* need help. "I'm a bit lost," I said.

"It's confusing down here, isn't it?" I nodded, and he pointed toward the open door. "Here's what to do. Go out and make a left. Walk all the way to the end of the corridor and make a right. You'll see a stairwell then."

"Thanks," I said. But I didn't move right away. I looked at Serena again. She was still turned around, looking at me, and she swiped at her face with a crumpled tissue.

"Do you need anything else?" the man asked.

"Um, I don't know," I said. It felt wrong to leave Serena all alone. Or, not all alone. Alone with a group of people I'd never seen before. None of them were in our grade at school. "Serena, are you okay?"

That was a dumb question. Of course she wasn't okay: she was crying.

"We're all fine, thank you," the man told me.

"Okay," I said.

I took a step back, still feeling unsure. That's when I heard the shout: "Lucy!"

It was Chloe's voice, followed by Theo's: "Lucy! Are you down here?"

"I think your search party has arrived," the man said.

I didn't respond. I just backed the whole way out of the room. Chloe and Theo were at the end of the corridor. I ran toward them, and they ran toward me, and we met in the middle.

"We were worried that you got sick," Chloe said.

"I'm not sick; I was just lost," I said, and then I whispered the next part: "But I saw a group of people down there." I pointed to the end of the hall. "Serena Kappas is with them."

"Who's Serena Kappas?" Chloe asked.

"A girl in our grade," Theo said. "In Mr. Goldfarb's class. I bet she's here for grief group."

"Grief group?" I asked.

"There were signs posted in the stairwell. Grief group meeting in room seventeen. Didn't you see?"

"No," I said. The things Serena had said pinged around in my brain. "Her mother didn't die, did she?"

"The week before last," Theo said.

Chloe gasped and brought a hand to her mouth. "I feel so badly for her," she said. "I don't even know her and I feel badly."

"I think you mean you feel *bad*," Theo said. "If you say you feel 'badly,' that means you're not good at feeling."

"But Chloe *is* good at feeling," I said. I turned to her. "Besides, I knew what you meant. I feel badly or bad or whatever the right thing to say is. I feel that, too."

"So do I," Theo said. "Serena and I were in preschool together, and our moms are still friends. Or, they were still friends."

"What happened to her?" Chloe asked.

"She had cancer," Theo said. "Not everyone dies of cancer. I've been reading a lot about it, and they have lots of treatments that work really well for people. But apparently Serena's mom had a really bad kind, and there wasn't any treatment for it. My parents went to the funeral."

Chloe made a little *ooh* sound.

"Serena's birthday is coming up," Theo continued. "Not this weekend but next. I heard my parents talking about it. Her mom was always big on birthdays, and Serena's dad doesn't know what to do. He's too sad himself."

"I can't imagine a birthday without my mom," Chloe

said. "That must be the worst thing ever." The instant the words were out of her mouth, her cheeks turned a deep red, the color of a Chanel dress I'd seen in *Vogue*'s Valentine's Day issue. "Oh my gosh, Lucy. I'm sorry."

"It's okay," I told her.

"I know your mom died, too. I didn't mean that it was the worst. I bet you have good birthdays, too."

"Yeah," I said.

"But I didn't mean it wasn't the worst, either, because I'm sure it's really hard sometimes. I just . . . I just don't know what to say. I shouldn't have said anything at all. I wasn't thinking."

I remembered how I'd made that comment about seeing cute animals, without thinking about how it could hurt Theo's feelings, since he couldn't get near them. I thought Chloe would never make a mistake like that, but maybe we all say things without thinking sometimes. I didn't want her to feel bad about it. "It's fine, really," I assured her. "It must be harder for Serena, because she's had her mom for ten years, and she was really used to it."

"Almost eleven," Theo said.

"Almost eleven," I repeated. "But my mom was only around for my first birthday. I've seen pictures, but I don't remember."

"We don't really have memories of things that happen before we know how to speak," Theo said. "It has to do with language acquisition. Basically, the words we learn code the memories to keep them in our brains."

"My mom sometimes forgets things, even though she's been able to speak for years. This morning she forgot where she'd left her keys," Chloe said.

"Really?" I asked. That made me feel better about Grandma.

"Yup."

"That's perfectly normal," Theo said. "There are only about six people in the world who can remember everything that ever happened to them. They have something called highly superior autobiographical memory. HSAM for short. But I bet they still needed language to start storing memories. It's too bad. I think it'd be cool to remember the first face you ever saw—which I guess would be the doctor who helped birth you."

"And it would be cool to remember the first time you tasted cake," Chloe said. "And the first joke you thought was funny."

"If you remember all the first happy things, you'd also remember the first sad things," I said.

"I suppose so," Theo said. "I don't think there's a filter for people with HSAM. I still think it'd be worth it."

"Yeah," I agreed. "I'd remember my mom."

"You sure you're okay?" Chloe asked.

"I am, I promise," I told her. "We should get going. You

know, before Valerie and Leesha think all three of us got sick or lost, or that we fell into the toilet."

I put an arm through Chloe's, so she'd know it really was okay. Then I linked my other arm through Theo's, and the three of us walked back upstairs.

CHAPTER 8

The next morning, Grandma made eggs for breakfast, and I told her all about Serena Kappas. "Theo said that Serena's mom was really into birthdays and always planned great parties."

"Poor girl," Grandma murmured.

"I know," I said. "But I have an idea."

"What's that?"

Before I could answer, Dad walked into the room. "Morning," he said. He had the newspaper tucked under his arm. Every morning of my life (except for the times he left for work before I woke up), that's been my first image of Dad: him entering the kitchen with the newspaper under his arm. He always gets a cup of coffee, and he drinks it standing up, paper propped open on the counter. I used to think that it was a very grown-up thing to do, but once when I tried to eat my breakfast at the counter, Grandma wouldn't have it. "Park your bottom on your seat, mago," she'd said.

As I could've predicted, Dad walked straight to the counter and poured himself a mug of the coffee Grandma had made. "Did you get my compliment card?" I asked him.

"What card?"

"I left it on your bedroom door."

I'd been leaving compliment cards for my family ever since we started the Kindness Club. Really, they weren't cards at all—just compliments written on Post-it notes, and stuck where they could find them. This latest one for Dad was my first kindness of the day. It said:

You're the best, Dad! Love, your favorite daughter, Lucy

"I didn't see it," Dad said.

Did it still count as my first kindness if the person the kindness was meant for didn't even read it?

Dad flipped the paper open on the countertop. "There are eggs still in the pan for you, Ken," Grandma said.

"Thanks, Ma. I'm not that hungry."

"You need to eat," she told him.

"Grandma says breakfast is the most important meal because it sets the tone for the rest of the day," I said.

"That's right," Grandma agreed.

"I'll take the eggs to go," Dad said, flipping a page.

"Ew, cold eggs," I said. "You should throw them out and buy something fresh when you get hungry."

"He can heat them up," Grandma said. "Waste not, want not." She stood and pulled open the drawer where we keep the Tupperware.

"What does that mean?" I asked.

"It means you should finish what's on your plate and not throw away perfectly good food," Dad said, his voice suddenly raised.

My cheeks went hot, as if I'd been slapped. "You know, that's the second time you've yelled at me this week when I haven't done anything wrong," I said.

"I wasn't yelling," Dad said. His voice was back to its usual decibel level, but it still had an edge to it.

"You *were* yelling," I insisted, and I turned to Grandma. "Wasn't he yelling?"

"Your father has a lot on his mind," she said, not answering the question. But I knew that meant I was right. "You only have to eat what you're hungry for."

"I'm done," I said, pushing my plate away. I hated fighting with my family. That's why I tried to never do it. But what had just happened with Dad wasn't my fault. "I hope you hire a replacement for Felix soon," I told him. "You must really be working too hard if you yelled at me about eggs. I just meant I wanted you to have a fresh meal. I was saying it to be *kind*."

"Yes, fine," Dad said. He folded the paper gruffly, like the paper had made him suddenly angry, too.

"You didn't tell me your idea for Serena," Grandma said.

"Oh, right. I almost forgot," I said. "I was thinking we could plan a birthday party for her. Chloe, Theo, and me. What do you think?"

"I think it's a lovely idea," Grandma said. "But keep in mind that Serena may not be in the mood to celebrate at all. This will be her first birthday without her mother."

"But that's exactly it," I told her. "Serena has memories of her mom on all her other birthdays, and I bet they're really good ones. But if we help her make new memories, then maybe her mom won't be the only thing on her mind. When I think of my birthday, I don't think of anyone missing. I think of you, and Oliver, and—" I broke off and glanced over at Dad, still standing by the counter. He was quiet, drinking his coffee, but his posture had softened a bit, like maybe he wasn't angry anymore. "And Dad," I finished up. "I think of all of you."

Dad put his coffee down and stepped over to the table. He put his hand on my head. I liked the feeling of it, heavy, a kind of hand-hat. He let it sit there for a couple seconds, and when he finally lifted it, he reached for my plate. "You're done, yes?"

"I am," I said.

He scraped my leftover eggs into the garbage, then turned on the tap to wash the plate by hand. It had only been two days since the dishwasher broke, and so far he and Grandma had been too busy to go to the store for a replacement.

"I can do that," Grandma said.

"Or I can," I said. "It's *my* plate."

"I'll take care of the dishes this morning," Dad said.

He didn't actually say "sorry" to me, but I took the dish washing, plus his hand-on-my-head moment, to mean that he was.

"Thanks, Dad," I told him.

"No problem."

"Don't you think it's a good idea?" I asked him. He looked puzzled, so I went on. "For my club to plan a birthday party for this girl in my grade whose mom just died. My birthday party at the bowling alley was my best birthday ever."

"We have had some nice memories at the bowling alley, haven't we?" he said.

"Oh yeah," I said. "Lots of them. That's why I think Serena would like a party there. Her birthday is next Sunday. That's such a good day for a party. You're rested up from the weekend, and you have one more fun thing to do before it's time for school. Don't you think?"

"Yes, sure."

"I love when my birthday falls on a weekend," I said. "I wish it happened every year."

"Lucy," Grandma broke in. "Take a look at the time."

The clock on the stove clicked from 7:38 to 7:39. Theo was going to be here any second. I had to be sitting at my desk in Ms. Danos's classroom in sixteen minutes. I ran upstairs to get my jacket, which had been part of Oliver's old marching band uniform. It had been way too big on me; but since he didn't need it anymore, he said I could do whatever I wanted to make it fit. I took in the back seam a couple inches and shortened the sleeves. It was blue, and I'd added some red fringe on the epaulets. The whole thing matched the T-shirt I was wearing, which incidentally I'd also made myself.

The breeze picked up as I marched down our front steps to the sidewalk. (When you're wearing a marching band jacket, you tend to march without even trying.)

"Don't worry, we'll be careful," Theo called.

"Careful about what?" I asked.

"He was saying it to appease me," came a voice from across the hedge.

"Oh, hi, Mrs. G!"

"Hello, young lady," she said. "You be careful, too, you hear? That's the kind of wind that could knock someone over and break their bones."

"I'll be fine, I promise," I told her.

"The storm last night undid your hard work, I'm afraid."

It was true. Chloe, Theo, and I had spent hours raking up a few years' worth of twigs and leaves scattered all over her front yard, and now it looked all messed up again. I bet things were worse in the backyard, where there were more trees for leaves to fall from.

"We have to go to school now, but I can clean things up when I get back."

"I'll be in the city this afternoon, if the weather cooperates."

"I can do it without you."

"Nonsense," Mrs. G said. "You come by this weekend, and we'll keep each other company."

"Okay," I said. "I will."

It was the weirdest thing—weird in a good way—that Mrs. G wanted my company at all. I used to think she was a witch, and she used to think I was a nuisance to the neighborhood. Now we were friends. It was all because of the Kindness Club, and it made me feel even more excited about our next project.

"Thanks, Mrs. G," I said. "I'll see you tomorrow."

CHAPTER 9

On the walk to school, I filled Theo in on my latest idea. He didn't seem quite as excited as I was about the whole thing—he didn't lift his knees high and march across Braywood School Road. (In fairness, he wasn't wearing a marching band jacket, just his usual khakis and a button-down, which was practically a uniform to Theo.) And he didn't wave enthusiastically at Kirby, the crossing guard, and shout out, "Have a wonderful day!" But, still, he said planning a party for Serena sounded like a good thing to do.

"We should talk to Serena at lunch today," I said as Kirby signaled it was safe for us to cross the street. "Next Sunday is only nine days away."

"It's more than a week."

"Yeah, but there's a lot to consider when planning a birthday party—or any kind of party."

It was a little like planning the perfect outfit—you needed

to decide theme, and colors, and whether you wanted everything to match just exactly, or whether you wanted it to be a
bit wackier and more original. I didn't know Serena well at
all, so I didn't know her taste.

"I want this to be the party of Serena's dreams," I went
on. "I want it to be *better* than anything she'd ever dreamed
of, so she'll remember it forever and play the movie in her
head for years to come."

"Did you know there's a German word for playing things
out in your head?" Theo asked. I shook my head. Of course
I didn't. "*Kopfkino*," he went on. "It translates to 'head
cinema.'"

By then we'd reached school, and Theo pulled open the
big red door.

"Why, thank you," I said, marching in ahead of him. We
had a couple of minutes left before the start of class, and
luckily Chloe was already there. I walked (okay, fine: marched)
over to her seat.

"Look at her," I heard Anjali say.

She was standing by Monroe's desk in the row behind
Chloe, and I knew she was talking about me. Sure enough,
Monroe called out, "Nice jacket, Lucy!" She was loud
enough that I was sure everyone in the room heard her,
including Ms. Danos, and it was clear by her tone that
Monroe didn't mean it as a compliment.

Here's something I figured out about kids and kindness—
kids learn to be kind at different speeds. It's like the reading

groups they put you in when you're in kindergarten. Some kids come to school already being great readers, and they're in the top group. That would've been Chloe when it came to kindness. Then there was Theo and me—at first we would've been put in the middle group, and after we met Chloe and started our club, we moved up to the top.

And, finally, there was Monroe Reeser. She'd be in the bottom group for kindness, and she wouldn't be moving up anytime soon. But every kid in my grade eventually learned to read. So maybe one day Monroe would learn to be kind, as well.

Or maybe not.

I took off my jacket and draped it across the back of my chair. My shirt was one I'd made myself. I'd taken an ordinary white shirt and cut the sleeves off. Then I'd sewed on a sleeve from a blue shirt on one arm, and a red shirt on the other. I'd worn it on the Fourth of July.

"My mom would never let me wear something like that," Monroe said loudly.

"Settle down," Ms. Danos said.

"I know the sleeves are lopsided," I told Chloe and Theo, softly so that the It Girls wouldn't overhear. "I took a risk and used different material on each sleeve."

If you don't take risks, you don't learn. You don't grow. You don't get better at things. That's what fashion has taught me.

I just wish I were able to skip over all the making-fun-of

parts, to the part when I'm already famous and Monroe Reeser is wearing my designs.

I wondered if kids gave Stella McCartney and Betsey Johnson a hard time when they were young. That was something I definitely planned to ask them about, when I grew up and got famous, too, and we all became friends.

"Just so you know, I like your outfit," Chloe told me. "Honestly, I really do. The jacket almost looks royal—like something the soldiers at Buckingham Palace would wear."

"The Queen's Guard," Theo said. "If the reigning monarch were a king, it would be called the King's Guard. Either way, their coats are red, not blue."

"It was Oliver's," I explained. "From when he was in the marching band."

"Cool," Chloe said. She lowered her voice to just a whisper. "Don't pay attention to what Monroe said."

"I'm not," I said. And I wasn't. Mostly, I wasn't. I knew that she and Anjali were still looking at me and snickering. But I kept my gaze laser-focused on Chloe and gave her a rundown of my idea for Serena's birthday.

"Oh wow," she said.

"I know. It's a perfect project for the club, right?"

"Perfect," she echoed. "But . . ."

"But what?"

"I've never met Serena. If you asked me to point her out in the cafeteria, I wouldn't be able to do it. Why would she want me at her birthday party if we're not friends?"

"Because—" I started.

"Okay, ladies and gentlemen," Ms. Danos said from the front of the room. "I need everyone in their own seats, please."

"Because planning her party will make you friends," I said quickly, and I scooted to the front row just as Ms. Danos closed the classroom door and told us to pass up our homework.

CHAPTER 10

They say variety is the spice of life, but that doesn't seem to be true when it comes to where people sit in the Braywood Intermediate School cafeteria. Every day, kids sit in the exact same seats as they did the day before, and the day before that, and so on and so on, as if cafeteria seats were assigned just like classroom ones. The difference is you get to sit with the people you want to sit next to.

I sit with Theo and Chloe, at a table smack in the middle of the room. Maybe it's a bit strange that we don't shake things up and switch seats each day, but the truth is, I like it the way that it is. It feels safe and cozy. A seat to go to, and friends who I know will sit beside me, day in and day out.

Before Chloe moved to town, it wasn't like that for me. I would pick up my lunch and look out over the sea of faces: who was friendly enough to sit with? Kids like Vanessa Medina and Serena Kappas were always nice about letting me sit with them. But it's not like they saved a seat for me, which made it feel like it wasn't really my seat after all.

I've heard lots of kids say that lunch is their favorite subject, but it was never mine. I like eating, and I like getting a break from classwork. But when you don't have your right place and your right friends, it's actually the worst time of day. It was like showing up to a fancy wedding in jeans. Everyone is looking at you. Everyone knows you don't belong. Now that I have my right spot, lunch is my favorite subject, too.

I put my tray down on the Kindness Club's regular table. Chloe sat on my side, like she always does, and Theo sat across. It was pizza day, and I tore off a piece of crust and popped it into my mouth. I always eat the crust first because it's my least favorite part, and I believe in saving the best for last.

"I don't think Serena is here yet," I said after I'd chewed and swallowed.

"Well, we just got here," Theo said. "Maybe Mr. Goldfarb's class isn't downstairs yet."

"No, they are," Chloe said. "I saw Rachael Padilla making a sandwich."

There was something about her tone—it sounded almost wistful. I worry sometimes that a part of Chloe still wants to be in the It Girls and sit at their table at the back of the room. Even though when she picked our club over theirs, Monroe told her in no uncertain terms that she would never make the mistake of being Chloe's friend again.

That was the exact word Monroe used—"mistake." It was such an awful thing to say, especially since being friends with Chloe is the total opposite of a mistake. But the point is, if a part of Chloe still wants to be friends with Monroe, then maybe a part of Monroe wants to be friends with Chloe, too.

"Hey, Chloe," I said. "Do you ever . . . well, I'm sure you don't . . . but do you ever miss Monroe and all them?"

"Yeah," Chloe said. "Sometimes I do."

"Really?" Theo asked.

"Well, yeah," she said. "It's not an everyday kind of missing them. Most of the time I don't. But every so often something will happen, and it'll make me remember something we did together. Like right now, eating pizza."

"That's not exactly a unique activity," Theo said. "Pizza is on forty percent of the menus in restaurants across the United States."

"Yeah, you're right," Chloe said. "It's just . . . I had some good times with them. Not like the times the three of us have, but still. I sometimes wish it had worked out differently and we could all be friends. I think it could've been fun."

"I think my gender prevents me from being a so-called It *Girl*," Theo said.

This conversation about Monroe and her friends had gone on too long. "Oh, enough about them," I broke in. "You know what will be even more fun? A birthday party for Serena." I stood up at my seat to have a better view of all the tables stretched out in front of me, but I didn't see her. So I turned around to look at the ones behind me—careful to avoid looking where I knew the It Girls would be. "If I were Serena, where would I be sitting?" I said.

"My guess is that she'll be sitting wherever Vanessa Medina is," Theo said. "Which is at the It Girls table, I'm afraid."

I didn't want to look, but I had to. And when I did, sure enough, there was Vanessa, right next to Monroe, in the exact seat where Chloe used to sit.

"I've never noticed Vanessa sitting with them before," I said. "What do you think she's doing there?"

Chloe shrugged. "They're looking for a new member," she said. "Because Monroe's best friend Haley moved away, and they wanted to have four people. It's better for when you pair off into things. That's why they were considering me."

"But Vanessa wouldn't leave Serena behind, would she?" I asked. "Especially not right after her mom died."

"I don't know," Chloe said. "I've never even met Vanessa."

"It'd be an awful thing for a best friend to do," I said. "I wonder if Serena would even want Vanessa at her birthday party."

"Maybe Serena wanted to sit somewhere else today," Chloe said. "Do you see her?"

"Nope," Theo said.

"Well, that explains it," Chloe said. "Vanessa sat there just because she didn't have Serena to sit with today."

You don't just sit with the It Girls because your usual friends aren't around. But I didn't say that out loud. Chloe knew that as well as I did.

I was still watching the table, and I saw Vanessa stand up and walk her tray over to the conveyer belt, where everyone drops their trays when they're done eating. Now was my chance. I picked up my own tray, walked as quickly as I could without spilling anything, and almost bumped into Vanessa as she turned around from the conveyer belt. "Oh, sorry," she said. "I didn't see you there."

"It's okay," I said. "I was actually coming to talk to you. Can I ask you something?"

"Is it about Serena's mom?"

"Sort of," I said. "Theo told me what happened. His mom was good friends with Serena's mom."

If I hadn't made friends of my own—real friends—and found a permanent table to sit at during lunch, I probably would've known before Theo told me. I would've been sitting with Serena and Vanessa, and maybe Serena would've told me what was happening, or Vanessa would've, right after. I felt bad that I hadn't known before. Not that there was anything I could do.

I was doing something now, though. I was planning a party.

"Is Serena in school today?" I asked.

"She was supposed to be," Vanessa said. "Daphne—that was Serena's mom's name—she died the week before last, and Serena said she'd be back this week. But then she decided to wait and start on Monday. I'm going over there after school to drop off her homework. If you have a message for her, I could tell her. Lots of people gave me messages to give her. Even a few teachers—even Principal Dibble."

"Anything about her birthday?" I asked.

"Her birthday?" Vanessa repeated. "No. That's not till next weekend, and I don't think she's thinking about it at all. Her family is pretty busy with other things."

"Of course," I said. "Good." Vanessa looked at me funny. "I mean, not good. Just . . . I just thought of something."

"What?"

I shook my head. "It's nothing much," I said. Even though of course it was something, and it was getting even better in my head. Serena was going to love it, I was sure. "When you see Serena, tell her I said hi," I told Vanessa. "Tell her I'll see her on Monday."

"Excuse me," a kid named Leon said. "You're blocking the line here."

Oops. I hadn't noticed, but there was a bit of a crowd gathering behind me, waiting to drop their own trays. "Sorry," I said. I scooted over. "Anyhoo," I said to Vanessa. "Will you tell her?"

"Sure," she said.

"Thanks."

I put my own tray on the conveyer belt. Then I headed back to Chloe and Theo, to report what had happened, and fill them in on my new-and-improved party idea.

CHAPTER 11

"Lucy! Watch it!"

It was Saturday morning. I'd gone to sleep thinking about Serena's party, and I'd woken up thinking about Serena's party.

"Sorry, Dad," I said. "I didn't see you there. But I'm glad I bumped into you. Guess what!"

"It's too early in the morning for guessing games," Dad said. "And you're going to hurt someone if you don't look where you're going."

"I said I was sorry," I told him. "Besides, it was just a coincidence that I opened my door at the exact same time you were walking by. Theo says the probability of coincidences is much higher than you'd think."

"Yes, well," Dad said, his voice coming out more grunt-like than word-like. "Okay, then."

He headed down the hall again, and so did I, since that's what I'd been planning to do all along. But even though we were going in the same direction, we weren't walking together. Dad stopped in the foyer long enough to grab his warm-up jacket, then opened the front door.

"'Bye," I called behind him, but he was already gone and didn't hear me.

Grandma was in the kitchen when I walked in, sitting at the table with her coffee, in the seat closest to the back window. She held the coffee mug between both hands and stared out at something in the backyard. "Hey, Grandma," I said.

She jumped in her seat, and the coffee sloshed a little bit. I grabbed a napkin from the counter to wipe it up. "Thanks. I didn't notice you came in."

"Dad didn't notice me before, either, and he nearly mowed me down. What were you looking at?"

"I was just thinking."

"About what?"

"Nothing," she said.

My grandmother never just sat and thought about nothing. She was always doing something. But people in my house were acting strange, not like themselves. It was as if something was in the water, changing their personalities.

But if it was the water, then my personality would be

changed, too. And I was perfectly fine. Something else was wrong. Something they weren't telling me.

"Are you okay?" I asked Grandma.

"Oh, sure, mago."

"Dad left," I told her.

"I know," she said. "He said he was going to head to the alley early today."

The words were barely out of her mouth when the front door opened again. "Who's that?" I asked.

"My best guess is your dad came back from something," she said. "Ken? Is that you?"

"Forgot my keys," Dad called back. We heard him thunder up the stairs, and a moment later, he thundered back down. I thought maybe he'd stick his head in the kitchen and say hi and good-bye, but he didn't. The front door opened and slammed shut again. He was gone.

Grandma had risen from her seat and took the used napkin from me. She wiped at some invisible spots on the counter, then folded it neatly.

"That's dirty," I said. "Shouldn't you throw it away?"

"I think it's got at least one more clean-up job in it," she said. "Breakfast?"

"I can make it."

I hunted around for the ingredients for a cheese omelet, but unfortunately we were out of the most essential ingredient—eggs. Instead, I poured Cheerios into two bowls, added milk, and set them on the table for Grandma and me.

"Thanks, mago."

"You're welcome," I said. "Hey, Grandma, Dad is too young to have Alzheimer's, right?"

"Oh, yes," she said. "Much too young. What has you thinking about Alzheimer's?"

"He forgot his keys."

"People forget keys all the time. It's perfectly normal."

"Yeah, that's what Theo said," I told her. "But his keys aren't the only thing Dad's forgetting."

"What else?"

"He's completely and totally forgotten how to be happy."

"Oh, mago, don't be hard on him."

"I'm not being hard. I'm being honest. He's been in a rotten mood all week. It's like he accidentally kicked his happiness under the bed, or stuck it in the bottom drawer or somewhere he can't even remember, like how Ollie lost his lucky marble last year, and it was in his winter coat pocket the whole time. All I know is Dad's usually a happy guy, and he's not anymore."

"Unfortunately, forgetting your happiness is also per-fectly normal sometimes—especially when you have a lot on your mind, which your father does." She lifted a spoonful of cereal to her mouth, but held it for a moment, still talking. "It would be interesting if emotions were physical objects, though, wouldn't it? You could put down your heartache and pick up your courage."

I nodded and swallowed my own spoonful of Cheerios. "Is Dad still upset because Felix left?" I asked.

"Mmm hmm," she said.

"Well, speaking of emotions," I said, "I'm mad at Felix, too. He worked for Dad for years. I thought they were friends. Why would he want to leave? How could he do that to Dad?"

"There are all sorts of reasons people have to leave their jobs. It's not personal."

"Sure it is," I said. "If you're friends with someone and you care about them, you should act like you do."

"It doesn't always work out that way," Grandma said. "Sometimes we act gruffly around those we care about the most."

"That doesn't make sense."

"I know, mago." Grandma reached toward me and flipped the "Designed by Lucy" tag under the collar. I was wearing what I always wore gardening. A green vest I'd made myself by taking the sleeves off an old jacket from Second Chance. "I love what you did with the patches on this."

"They're not just patches," I told her. "They're pockets for gardening tools, or candy for energy, or whatever you might need when you're working in someone's yard. I'm going over to Mrs. G's as soon as I finish breakfast."

"Oh, no," she said. "It's too early to go over to anyone's house. You need to wait till a respectable hour."

"When's that?"

"I'd say ten."

"Ten? That's practically three hours away!"

"Okay, nine thirty. But not a minute sooner. Do you want me to cut a banana into your cereal?"

"No, thanks."

"All right, then." She stood and brought her bowl to the sink. "If you're all set here, I'll get going."

"Wait a second," I said. "You're going out now, but I'm not allowed to?"

"I'm doing inventory at Quinnifer's, and then I'm meeting your dad at the alley. Promise me you won't bother Mrs. Gallagher until nine thirty."

"Mrs. G wouldn't think it was a bother, because I'm helping her, which she asked me to do, by the way. She even said I should do it this weekend—and the weekend starts right now."

"Lucy—" Grandma started.

"It's fine," I cut her off. "I'll wait, I promise."

"Good girl. I'll see you later, mago." She gave me a little peck on the top of my head.

"'Bye, Grandma," I said.

I didn't know what to do with myself to fill the time, but since our yard had gotten messed up from the storm, I decided to start there. It'd been a bit chilly when I walked outside, but soon I was all warmed up. By the time I was finished loading leaves into garbage bags, I figured it was nine thirty, or close enough. And even if it wasn't, I could get started on Mrs. G's yard without her actually helping me. I pulled Grandma's wheelbarrow out of the shed and headed over to Mrs. G's to get to work.

"Well, hello there, Lucy!" Mrs. G called a while later. I looked up to see her at the kitchen window. She used to throw the window open and yell at me to get off her property—back when I'd never even stepped foot on her property and I was on the sidewalk, which belonged to everyone, but she acted like she owned it. Now I *was* in the middle of her yard, and she was smiling. "You're up bright and early today," she said.

I leaned against the rake and wiped my brow. "I'm almost done out here," I said. "But I still need to do the backyard. Lots of leaves must've fallen off that big oak you have."

"They sure did," she said. "But why don't you come inside and take a break first? Did you eat yet? I have some fresh cookies inside."

"Cookies for breakfast?"

"Can you think of a better meal?"

I shook my head. Adults can really surprise you sometimes. "No, I can't," I said. "I'm coming!"

Mrs. G's kitchen was painted a dull yellow, the color of a shirt that's been washed a few hundred times. A small wooden table was pushed up against the wall, under a window framed by faded floral drapes. The two chairs had matching floral cushions, and a bowl of apples sat in the center of the table. There was something about the apples—they looked almost too perfect. I reached out to one.

"They're plastic," Mrs. G said. "Just for decoration. I have some figs in the fridge if you're craving fruit."

"No, thank you," I said in my most polite voice. I'd never had a fig before, and I was pretty sure I never wanted to, but I didn't want to be rude about it. "I'd much rather have a cookie, if you don't mind."

"I don't mind at all," she said.

Before we started the Kindness Club, I may have just sat at the table waiting to be served. Now I wanted to help Mrs. G get things ready. But it was hard because I didn't know my way around her kitchen. I opened a drawer that was filled with about fifty napkin rings. "Uh, do we need these?" I asked.

"No," she said. "Just take a seat." I did, and watched as she pulled a couple mismatched plates from a shelf. She brought them over to the table, along with a bakery box. "The clerk at the bake shop put a little piece of bread in to keep them fresh," she told me as she fiddled with the white ribbon. "Do you know that trick?"

"Nope."

"The cookies absorb the moisture from the bread and stay soft. The bread gets hard, but that's fine because it's not the bread that we want to eat, is it?"

I shook my head. "No offense, bread," I said, addressing the bread as if it were a living thing that had feelings. "It's not your fault that cookies taste so much better."

"They do indeed," Mrs. G said. "Aha! Got it!" She untangled the ribbon and tipped the box toward me. "These are the treats Thomas would buy when he was courting me. Take one."

I reached for a peanut butter cookie, but then I hesitated. "I don't want to pick your favorite."

"Don't worry, dear," Mrs. G said. "I like them all."

So I took my peanut butter cookie, and Mrs. G took a double chocolate one. "What's 'courting' mean?" I asked.

"It's an old-fashioned way of saying you're trying to get someone to like you. Thomas and I were lawyers at the same firm. For months he found excuses to stop by my desk and ask me questions that he already clearly knew the answer to, until he finally asked the question he really wanted to ask— would I go out with him."

"And you said yes?"

"Apparently I did."

"That's funny you were lawyers, because 'courting' sounds like a lawyer thing to do. Get it? Because lawyers have to go to court?"

"I do," Mrs. G said. "But I never thought about that

until just now. You know, back then there were a lot of male lawyers in the firm that felt I should quit or be fired, so my position could be given to a deserving *man*."

"But that's crazy!" I said. "The position should go to the most deserving *person*."

"I agree," Mrs. G said. "I worked hard to get that job. But Thomas was always kind to me. He was my friend. When we decided to get married, he left the firm because it was frowned upon to have both spouses working there. I stayed on for a while, and more women were hired. It was slow at first. But if you look at the list of lawyers working at my old firm now, there are just as many women as men."

"So things changed," I said. "That's cool."

"It is," she said. "Change is an interesting thing, don't you think?"

"I don't really like change," I admitted. "I mean, I'm glad things changed with us and we're friends now, and I'm glad things changed at your law firm. But other than that, I like when things stay the way you expect them to. That's why I kept my old room and let Ollie keep his."

"I understand," Mrs. G said. "But eventually everything changes. It's just what happens. We need to accept it in all forms. One day, years from now, you'll be walking down Main Street and you'll remember the way it all looked when you were—how old are you now? Ten?"

"Yes."

"Fifth grade," she said, and I nodded. "You'll remember

exactly what it looked like when you were ten and in fifth grade, and it will seem like yesterday to you, and all the young ones around you will think you're ancient for feeling that way. They'll take everything new for granted, and they'll think it'll always stay that way. But you'll be older and wiser and you'll know that things change. It makes everything you're doing more important and less important, both at the same time. Thomas and I used to walk down to Main Street on weekend mornings and wave to the seamstress in the window of J's Cleaners."

"I don't know J's Cleaners," I said.

"It's gone now," Mrs. G said. "Long gone. The owners moved down to Florida and it became a video store, which Thomas loved, by the way. He'd pick up a new movie for us to watch every Saturday night. But now the video store is gone, too. People stopped renting them."

"I watch movies on my computer," I told her.

"Ah," Mrs. G said. "I don't even have one of those."

"You don't?"

"I never felt the need. When I was young, computers hadn't even been invented yet. Every time I think everything has already been invented, there is something new on the market. Can you imagine all the things that will exist when you grow up that don't exist now?"

I shrugged. "I'll have to ask Theo. I bet he'll invent at least a hundred things himself."

"Do you want another cookie?"

"Yes, please."

I picked a chocolate chip one this time, and Mrs. G had an oatmeal raisin. She took a bite and closed her eyes as she chewed and swallowed. "All this talk of change," she said, her eyelids popping open again. "And yet this cookie tastes exactly the way I remember it tasting when Thomas first bought one for me, fifty-seven years ago."

"Fifty-seven years is a long time," I said. "You must have a lot of memories of him."

"I do."

"Do you remember things about your birthdays?"

"Yes. Birthdays and ordinary days. There's a lot to remember."

"Isn't it weird that once a day is done, it's done?" I asked. "I'll never have the exact same day ever again. This is the only day of this week of this year that I'll ever have."

"Lucy," Mrs. G said, "you are what my husband would've called an old soul."

"Is that a good thing?" I asked.

"It certainly is. It means you're wise beyond your years. And I'll tell you another thing—if this is the only day of this week of this year that I'll ever have, then I'm glad I'm spending part of it with you."

"Me too," I said.

We were each quiet for a few seconds, finished up our

second cookies. I could hear the *click-click* of my own chewing. I swallowed and said, "There's another weird thing I think about sometimes."

"What's that?"

"Well, here we are having a good day. We even have cookies. But all around the world, other people are having their own days—some of them might be having good days, too, but some of them are having bad ones. It feels wrong to enjoy things when you know lots of people are having bad luck things happen."

"Parallel lives, Thomas used to call it," Mrs. G said. "We're all here on the same planet, living lives next to one another, but not the same lives. You can never tell what is going on in someone else's life."

"There's a girl in my grade who I *know* is having a bad day. Her name is Serena Kappas, and her mom just died."

"It must make you feel sad about your own mother to think of Serena losing hers," Mrs. G said.

"Yeah, it does," I said. "But I think it's more like you and your husband, and the way you remember him and talk about him. Serena is ten now, like me, so obviously she knows lots of words, way more than I did when my mom died, and that means she can keep her memories. If she remembers her mom a lot, she must miss her so much."

"Yes, I'm sure she does."

"I overheard her talking about her mom's clothes, and she even misses those. Her aunt gave them all to a thrift store.

I bet it was Second Chance, since that's the only one in town. Now all her mom's stuff is gone, but Serena wanted to keep everything."

"I'm sure her aunt felt she was doing the right thing," Mrs. G said. "It's hard to know what that is sometimes. People grieve in different ways. They have different needs to get them through it."

"I didn't even tell you the worst part yet—Serena's birthday is next weekend."

"I'm sure that will be very hard for her."

"I know," I said. "Theo said that Serena's mom was really into birthdays. Serena's best friend said no one else is planning anything this year. They've all been too distracted. But that's okay, because I'm going to plan a surprise party for her. The three of us will—Chloe, Theo, and me. After all, this will be the only eleventh birthday that Serena will ever have. I asked my dad and he said we can do it at Tanaka Lanes."

"That's sweet of you, Lucy," Mrs. G said. "And generous of your dad. But before you get too deep into the plans, I think you should call *Serena's* dad and make sure it's all right. He may be planning something private."

"But her best friend would know about it—even if it was private."

"Very well," Mrs. G said. "Then he may not be planning anything because Serena herself decided that she didn't want to commemorate the day."

"I thought about that," I said. "But what if she told her dad she doesn't want a party?"

"Then you shouldn't have one."

"But she *would* want this one," I told Mrs. G. "I just know she would—even if she doesn't know it yet herself. Once it happens it'll be great."

"Asking her father is still the right thing to do," Mrs. G said. "And he may say yes. You don't know."

"I don't have Serena's number."

"We can look it up."

"You don't have a computer," I reminded her.

"That's right," she said. "I'm probably the last person on the planet without one."

"Not on the planet. In social studies Ms. Danos said fifteen percent of people in the United States don't have one. There are probably people in other countries, too."

"I suppose I'm not the last person on the planet. Perhaps just the last in Braywood."

"So how will I get the number to call?"

"My dear," Mrs. G said. "It's called a phone book. Come on, I'll show you."

CHAPTER 12

I had the phone in my hand, and the phone book opened in front of me. I traced a finger down the names listed alphabetically in teeny-tiny black letters, and I found them at the bottom of the page. KAPPAS, Alec & Daphne.

Daphne. Serena's mom's name. I'd heard Vanessa say it, and there it was. Printed in the phone book like she was still alive.

"You all set?" Mrs. G asked.

I nodded and began to dial. But then I pressed the button to hang up. "What if Serena herself answers. Then what do I say?"

"You would say, 'Can I please speak to Mr. Kappas?'"

"Okay."

"Or if you think Serena may recognize your voice, you can say hello and tell her you were just calling to check in."

"I don't think she will," I said. "We're not really friends."

"Oh?"

"We're not enemies or anything," I said quickly. "She was always nice to me. She let me sit with her at lunch, even when other people didn't want me to."

"You're acquaintances, then," Mrs. G said.

"Yeah, I guess so. Some people might not want Chloe, Theo, and me at their birthday party, but I don't think Serena will mind. She's pretty kind herself. Plus, we'll invite all her friends."

"This party is a very kind thing for you to do," Mrs. G said. "Especially for someone you don't know well."

"Thanks." I looked back down at the phone book and dialed the Kappases' number. The phone rang once, twice. I started to think maybe no one was home.

But then: "Hello?"

It was a woman's voice. My eyes flashed to Mrs. G. We hadn't discussed what I'd say if neither Serena nor her father answered. I wished we'd scripted the whole thing out before I'd dialed. It was like when I get excited about a new design, and I start cutting and sewing before I sketch things out. It's almost always a mistake.

"Hello?" the woman on the other end repeated. "Hello?"

"Um, hello," I said finally. "I'm calling for Mr. Kappas."

"He's not in," the woman said. "This is his sister. May I help you with anything?"

"You're Mr. Kappas's sister," I said. "Serena's aunt?"

"Yes."

"Aunt Odessa?"

"The one and only. Are you one of Serena's friends?"

"I go to school with her. We're not in the same class, but I know what happened to her mother, and I'm very sorry."

"We are all very sorry," Serena's aunt agreed. "It's sweet of you to call, uh . . . What did you say your name was?"

"I didn't. It's Lucy Tanaka."

"Well, Lucy Tanaka, I don't know if Serena is available right now, but I can check."

"No!" I said quickly. "I mean, no, thank you. You see, I have a surprise for Serena. A *maybe* surprise—I wanted to cheer her up, but I wanted to ask her dad if it was okay first."

"You can ask me. I'm handling a bunch of things around here."

"Okay, well, I talked to Vanessa Medina. Do you know her?"

"She's another friend of Serena's."

"Right," I said. "They're best friends, and I asked Vanessa if Serena was doing anything for her birthday, and Vanessa said she didn't think anything had been planned."

"There isn't anything planned," Aunt Odessa said. "I haven't been able to get Serena to talk about it."

"I thought maybe I could plan something," I said. "My friends and I want to. My dad owns Tanaka Lanes."

"The bowling alley?"

"Yup."

"No wonder your name sounded familiar to me. It's on Sheridan Road, right?"

"Yeah, and they do really cool things for birthday parties. I asked my dad, and he said we could do the same for Serena. I thought we could make it a surprise, to distract her from everything else that's happened."

"Well, aren't you a sweetheart," Aunt Odessa said.

"So does that mean yes?" I asked. "You wouldn't have to help with anything, except maybe getting Serena to Tanaka Lanes next Sunday."

"Of course I can do that. It would be my pleasure."

I grinned at Mrs. G and gave her a thumbs-up sign. "Great," I said into the phone. "Don't tell Serena. I want to surprise her."

"I won't, I promise. And Lucy?"

"Yes?"

"Thank you. Thanks a lot."

CHAPTER 13

As soon as I hung up with Serena's aunt, I called Theo to tell him the news. He sounded excited. Well, excited *for Theo*. He doesn't exactly jump up and down and shriek the way I do sometimes. But in his Theo-way, I could tell he was pleased. "How many people are we expecting?" he asked.

"I haven't figured it out yet," I said. "There are the three of us, plus Serena and Vanessa." I looked over at Mrs. G. "Do you want to come, too?" I asked her.

"I'm not really a bowler, dear," Mrs. G said. "But I appreciate the invitation."

"Okay, not Mrs. G," I said to Theo. "But I'm thinking Serena's aunt will want to be included, maybe her dad, too, and her other friends besides just Vanessa. Do you know who they are?"

"Social groups are not really my area of expertise," Theo

said. "I would say that Serena seems to be one of those peo-ple whom everyone likes."

Whom: only Theo would use the word "whom" in a sen-tence, when it wasn't for one of Ms. Danos's grammar work sheets.

But there were an extra couple of words he wasn't using: Serena seems to be one of those people whom everyone likes—*unlike us.*

I shook it off. It didn't matter to me. I had my friends, and Serena had hers, and we'd all be together for her birthday.

"We'll do a little research this week and find out who her friends are," I said.

"How many people on a bowling lane?" Theo asked.

"My dad likes to have six, which is the maximum," I told him. "But the truth is it's better if you have no more than four, because then you don't have to wait too long to take a turn."

"So we should try to invite a multiple of four," Theo said.

Leave it to Theo to be really scientific about it.

"I guess it depends on how many friends she has," I said. "But we can try. Want to come over and start planning?"

"No, thank you," Theo said. "My parents went out, and Anabelle is doing something with her track team. So this is my alone time. You understand, right?"

"Why do you want alone time? I had so much of it before we started the club, and so did you. You don't want to go back to that, do you?"

"No, of course not," Theo said. "But I like having a balance. Club time, and alone time. They're both important to me."

"I think alone time is more important to you than it is to me," I said.

"It's because I'm an introvert," Theo explained. "I need to have time to myself, to get reenergized. You're more of an extrovert. You get energized around people."

"Yeah, I totally do," I agreed. "Call me if you decide you've had enough alone time."

"I will," Theo promised.

When I hung up with Theo, I wanted to call Chloe and fill her in on everything, too. She was at her dad's house for the weekend, and I didn't know his number by heart. I couldn't look it up in the phone book because he doesn't live in Braywood, so his number wouldn't be listed. (Well, I'm sure it was listed in some phone book, but not in the one at Mrs. G's house.)

But as soon as I got home, I grabbed the phone from the kitchen and ran up to my room. The phone number was on a Post-it Chloe had given me, back when we first became friends.

Now, Chloe is the type of person who can be jumpy and shrieky like me. Maybe not quite as much as me, but pretty close. Probably because she's an extrovert, too. We cheered together over the phone, and then we started to talk plans, but in the background her dad called to her that it was time to get going. "Sorry," she told me. "We're headed out to go apple picking with Gloria and Sage. Don't do too much planning without me, okay?"

I said okay, even though all I wanted to do was party plan right then. But luckily I remembered I was in the middle of another project. It wasn't quite as exciting as making a birthday party for Serena, but it was still pretty great: the Community House quilt. I'd nearly forgotten about it, but I bet the patches the kids had made were all completely dried. I just had to pick them up and sew them together, and voilà! A quilt!

I changed out of my gardening clothes into pedal-pusher jeans (regular-length jeans that I'd hemmed myself) with a bandanna belt (three bandannas I'd sewn together) and called Grandma to tell her where I was headed. She didn't answer her cell phone, so then I tried Tanaka Lanes. But the woman who answered said both Grandma and Dad were in a meeting and unavailable. "Do you know how long the meeting will be?" I asked.

"I'd guess it'll be a while. An hour or two at least."

"Okay. Thanks."

I pressed the button to hang up. I wasn't supposed to go anywhere without telling one of them first. Now what?

Oh. Oliver!

Back before he'd left for college, Oliver was left in charge of me a lot, and I went to him for permission to do things. Just because there were a couple hundred miles between us now didn't make him any less grown-up. In fact, these days he was even *more* grown-up—he was older than he ever had been before; and for that matter, so was I.

He answered: "Hey there, your royal goose-ness," he said.

"Hi!" There were muffled voices in the background. Oliver lives in a dorm. Every room in his building has two people living in it. There are bathrooms down the hall, which everyone shares, plus a big room in the center called a "common room," where people hang out, watch TV, play games, that sort of thing. From the sound of the voices, I wondered if that's where he was. "I have a favor to ask," I said.

"How can I be of use, Ms. Goose?"

"First of all, you're a poet and you didn't even know it."

"Oh, I know it."

"And second," I went on, "I want to go to the Community House to pick up a quilting project, but Grandma and Dad are both in a meeting at the bowling alley. I can't ask their permission to leave the house, so I'm asking for yours instead. Do I have it?"

"Hmm," Ollie said, and I could practically see him twiddling his fingers just to torture me. "I don't know. You could get into a lot of trouble at the Community House."

"Oh, come on. Please. I'll be super quick. I just need to pick something up. It's for my club."

"The Kindness Club?"

"Yup, that's the one."

"Well, in that case, I guess I can't say no."

"Oh, thank you, Ollie. Thanks a lot!"

"Hang on," he said. "I have a few rules. First, go straight to the Community House. Second, come straight home. Also leave a note for Grandma and Dad before you go, and call me the minute you walk back in the door. I'd say it'd take about fifteen minutes for you to walk there, fifteen minutes to do whatever you need to do, and fifteen minutes to get home. So you better call me in forty-five minutes. Got it?"

"I got it," I said. "Thanks again."

"I'm happy to be back in charge," Ollie said.

"Who's letting you be in charge, Ollie?" I heard someone say—a girl.

"My kid sister," he replied. He'd never called me his "kid sister" before. He'd just said "sister," or sometimes "little sister." I didn't like the term "kid." It made me feel younger than I was, like someone who wasn't old enough to be his best friend.

"Who are you talking to?" I asked him.

"Just a friend," he said.

"A *girl*friend?" I asked.

"Well, she's a girl, and a friend," he said. Behind the words, I could hear someone giggling—probably the same girl.

"Come on, is she?" I asked.

"That's for me to know and you to find out."

"When?"

"When I say so."

He had a secret from me. I couldn't remember him keeping a secret from me before. Best friends don't do that. Except I was wondering if Ollie had changed his mind about that. Mrs. G had been right about things changing.

"I think it's so cute that you're talking to your little sister," I heard the girl say.

"Ollie?"

"Listen," he said. "You have your errand to run, so I'm going to sign off. Don't forget to call me when you get home. And leave a note for Grandma and Dad before you go. And CALL ME."

"I'll do all those things, I promise. I'll never let you down because you're my best friend."

"Good girl, Lucy-goose-alicious. I'll talk to you later."

CHAPTER 14

The big room at the Community House was being used as a yoga studio when I got there, which meant I had to wait for twenty-three minutes. I walked the length of the orange and yellow hallway, feeling nervous. What if someone mistook the patches for garbage and threw them away? What if I took too long to call Oliver and he called the police?

I couldn't do anything about the potential first problem, but as far as the second problem was concerned, I'd have to run all the way home. I didn't want to risk worrying my brother, and I certainly didn't want to risk police involvement!

Okay, that problem was solved. Now back to the first one: worrying about the patches. I'd paced the length of the hallway to the front door and turned to walk back down again. I began to count my steps. *If the last step is on an even number, the patches will be there*, I told myself.

Thirty-one.

Thirty-two.

Thirty—

The door at the end of the hall was pushed open by a woman, hair slicked back with sweat, yoga mat under her arm. I jogged the last few steps to the door, losing track of what step number I was on, and headed inside. There were a couple dozen women and a couple of guys with their own rolled-up yoga mats standing around talking to one another. One woman was in the center of them all. She was wearing layered tank tops, pink on the bottom and black on top, and zebra-print leggings. She had to be the one in charge, because she had a headset on like a concert singer.

I walked past her and everyone else, and headed over to the windowsill. No patches. My heart picked up its pace, but I took a couple calming breaths.

"Hey, do you need help with something?" one of the women asked. She'd broken away from the group to come over to me. "Are you looking for your mom?"

People always assume kids have moms. I guess that's understandable, since most kids do. But I don't, and so it always gives me a little tingle when people ask me about mine.

"No," I said quickly. "I'm just looking for some patches."

"Patches?" she asked, confused.

"The kids in the after-school program decorated them. They were right here. Did you see if anyone put them somewhere?"

"No," she said. "But I'm not sure you should be taking anything from the after-school program out of this room."

I was aware time was tick-ticking by. Oliver would expect me to be home in five minutes. Even if I left now and ran the whole way, I was cutting it very close. But luckily I didn't have to waste time assuring her that I wasn't a thief, because someone called out my name: "Lucy!"

I turned around. "Leesha. Thank goodness you're here."

"I never miss Laura's yoga class," she said, nodding toward Zebra-Pants Headset Woman. "We use this room because it's the biggest, and she always draws a crowd. You should come sometime."

"I will," I said. "But for now I came to pick up the patches so I can make the quilt like I promised."

"I put them in the supply closet for safekeeping. Come with me."

The supply closet was in the corner of the little-L part of the room. Leesha took out the stack of dried patches and slipped them into a manila envelope.

"Thanks," I said. "I gotta run home now."

"'Bye," she called.

I'm sure I beat some sort of world record on the way home, and I was panting when I dialed Oliver, who didn't even pick up the phone, so I left a message: "It's me, your favorite sister and BFF. I'm home safe and sound, and I'm going to stay

here now and make my quilt. Hope you're having fun with
your *girlfriend*."

Since my bedroom is so small, I keep my sewing machine
in a corner of the living room. I pulled it out and turned it
on. I love the sound it makes when it hums to life, a gentle
kind of whirr, like the sound of a hummingbird's fragile little
wings flapping. I loaded a spool of white thread onto the spool
pin. Then I realized I had a problem. The kids' patches were
all different shapes. I'd done it to make it more fun and creative for them. But it turned out I'd presented an extra challenge for myself. You'd think with the experience I have
designing and sewing my own things, I would've figured that
out *before* I sat down to stitch the quilt together.

But I thought of a solution: I'd sew each of the kids' differently shaped patches onto carefully measured square
patches, then I'd sew all of them together. I needed to
save the flat sheet for the back of the quilt. Luckily, I had
some of the fitted-sheet fabric left over, as well as the pillowcases. I got out a tape measure and fabric scissors, but
before I got to work measuring and cutting, I had another
inspired idea. Tie-dye.

YES, TIE-DYE!

The sheets and pillowcases from Anabelle were white
and, like blank pieces of paper, they'd been perfect for the kids
to decorate. But they'd make pretty boring squares . . . unless
I spiced things up a bit. In fact, I'd also dye the flat sheet and
spice up the back of the quilt, too.

I had tie-dye supplies left over from the summer. Within twenty minutes, I was in the backyard (where Grandma had made a rule that all tie-dyeing was to take place) with one bucket of blue dye and another of red. I'd folded the sheets and pillowcases accordion-style, and wrapped rubber bands around them. Every two to three inches, another rubber band. Then, wearing Grandma's kitchen gloves, I dunked the pillowcases and fitted sheets into the red dye, and the flat sheet into the blue. When they finished soaking, I undid the rubber bands, and turned on the backyard hose to rinse them super thoroughly. Finally I was done.

Well, not exactly done. It was time to put the sheets in the washing machine. By then, Grandma had come home for dinner. She made stir-fry veggies and tofu over rice, and put a plate in the fridge for Dad to eat when he got home, whenever that was. Midway through the meal, the washing machine beeped, and I switched the sheets to the dryer.

After we cleaned up, Grandma offered to help me cut the red tie-dyed fitted sheet and pillowcases into perfect squares. She went into her room to get her reading glasses. You need to see well to make sure the cuts are precise as they need to be. When she didn't come out within a few minutes, I went looking for her. She was lying on her bed, still clothed. Her eyes were closed, and her reading glasses were on the end table.

My breath caught in my throat, and my eyes zeroed in on her chest. It was moving up and down, up and down, just like it was supposed to. She was alive, just tired, and that was fine. I didn't mind cutting the squares on my own. But it wasn't like her to go to sleep so quickly after dinner. Another weird symptom of something I couldn't pin down.

I found a Post-it and scribbled a message to stick on Grandma's door, for her to find in the morning:

Dinner was delicious. I hope you wake up well rested and all better!

Then I went back to the other room and got to work.

CHAPTER 15

I spent a couple hours on Saturday night and all day Sunday on the quilt (minus the time I went back to Mrs. G's to rake up the leaves in her backyard).

After I cut the red squares, I fired up my sewing machine (aka, pressed the button to turn it on). I used white thread to sew the kids' patches on, because I didn't want the stitches to show. Of course they would a little bit, but I wanted the stitches to be as invisible as possible.

The patches came out looking a little bunched up once they were attached to the red tie-dyed backing. I tried to iron them down. Ironing is just about my least favorite task. I've burned myself twice. But if you're going to work in fashion, you have to accept that wielding a hot iron is at least occasionally going to be a part of your life.

The ironing only partly worked to make the patches lie flat. It wasn't perfect, which was a bit disappointing. Stitching the squares together went more smoothly, and once that was done, I turned the whole thing facedown and matched it up to the edges of the big, tie-dyed blue sheet. I sewed three quarters of the edges together, then I turned it inside out, which is called "envelope style," and stitched the last edge together with teeny-tiny yellow stitches.

When she came in to say good night on Sunday, Grandma admired the finished quilt draped across the top of my dresser.

"It's not as thick as I expected it to be. I don't know why I thought two sheets sewn together would look thicker in the end. How did the pioneers keep warm under quilts like this?"

"I think the point is they didn't keep warm," Grandma said. "But not to worry. This quilt is for decoration at the Community House, not for practical use. And it looks great."

"It's not perfect."

"Oh, mago," Grandma said with a sigh. "If you're searching for perfection you're always going to let yourself down. It's a perfectly good quilt. You should be proud."

By Monday, I was back in school and ready to tackle the next kindness project: Serena's birthday party. Chloe and Theo met me after Ms. Danos had let our class go for lunch. Chloe was clutching a brown paper bag. "Did you bring your lunch to school?" I asked.

"Nope," she said. "It's a little surprise for you guys."

"What is it?" Theo asked.

"I'm not telling you yet," she said. "That's why it's called a surprise."

"Well, speaking of surprises," I said, and I lowered my voice in case Serena was nearby. "I think we should find Serena in the cafeteria and invite her to sit with us."

"She always sits with Vanessa," Theo said.

"Fine, so we'll invite Vanessa, too."

Of course it was possible that Vanessa would want to sit with the It Girls, but I didn't mention that. Neither did Chloe or Theo. We rounded the corner. The hot-lunch line had already formed and stretched into the corridor. A few kids jogged ahead of us to get a closer spot. "But I thought her party was going to be a surprise."

"Right," I said. I was practically whispering at that point. "But none of us know her that well, so we should still try to find out what would make the perfect party for Ser . . . for Petunia."

"Who's Petunia?" Theo asked.

"It's a code name," I said. "Now we can talk about this safely."

Theo rolled his eyes, but Chloe said, "Good idea." Then she paused. "But how will we get that information from *Petunia* without ruining the surprise for her?"

"We'll be really crafty about it," I said. "I'm crafty after all."

"You are?"

"I made this skirt," I said, shaking my hips a little so Chloe could see better how I'd sewn together panels from four different shirts I'd grown out of but hadn't wanted to part with.

"Right, of course," she said.

"Being good with textiles doesn't necessarily equate to being crafty in other forms," Theo said. "Especially with things that don't involve physical materials."

"Huh?" I asked, which is, incidentally, a word I use an awful lot around Theo. In fact, I'd probably said "huh" more in the last few weeks of being his friend than I did in all the other weeks of my life put together.

"I just mean being good at sewing doesn't mean you're particularly clever at getting someone to give you details about her life, without knowing *why* she's giving you the details," he explained. "Not that you're not clever; I just mean there's no correlation between one kind of crafty and the other."

"Well, in this case there is," I told him.

By then we'd made it to the front of the lunch line, and we each got a plate of veggie chili. I topped mine with a little bit of sour cream and a lot of grated cheese. "Keep your eyes peeled for Petunia," I said.

And we all did, but we didn't see her, not as we picked up utensils, or stopped at the water dispenser, or headed across the room to our table.

Four people we *did* happen to see were the three It

Girls, plus Vanessa, back at their table. "Maybe Serena's not in school again," Chloe said.

"Maybe," I said. I blew on a spoonful of chili to cool it down. "Maybe you should try calling her later," I told Theo.

"Me?" he asked. "Why me?"

"You know her best."

"I barely know her at all," he said. "You're the one who used to have lunch with her."

"Yeah, but we weren't really friends. Just acquaintances. Unlike your mom and her mom."

"Yes, but I'm not crafty like you," he said.

I had to laugh, but I cut myself off when I spotted Serena out of the corner of my eye. "Look!" I said. "There she is!"

"Where?" asked Chloe. "I don't know what she looks like, remember?"

"She's in a striped shirt, and her hair comes almost down to her waist. And she's walking out of the lunchroom right now." I pushed back my chair so quickly it wobbled.

"Careful!" Chloe called.

"I'm fine," I told her, standing quickly. "I'm going to ask Serena to sit with us."

I crossed the room as fast as I could. Serena was holding a cafeteria tray with chili, no toppings, and a plain roll. Hot lunch. According to the rules Chloe had once told us, It Girls weren't allowed to eat the hot lunch. Maybe that meant Serena wouldn't even be allowed at their table.

"Hey," I said when I'd caught up with her. She stopped

in her tracks and turned to me. I'd never noticed before, but she had the greenest eyes I'd ever seen. I decided to say something about them—a compliment card spoken out loud, because I needed something to break the ice. "Your eyes are really pretty," I told her.

"Oh. Thanks."

Then I didn't know what to say. Should I tell her I was sorry to hear that her mom had died? I was, obviously, but it was hard to know what to do. What if she wasn't thinking about her mom right then, and I reminded her what had happened and made her feel sad in a moment when she'd been feeling okay? That seemed like the opposite of kindness.

There was a silence between us, but it was my turn to speak so I had to say something. "You know Theo Barnes, right?" I asked.

"Yeah," she said. "His mom was friends with my mom."

Her eyes clouded over, and I knew it was my fault. I'd mentioned her mom without even trying. In fact, I was purposely trying not to. But there we were, talking about a mom she no longer had. It made me feel like the woman at the Community House: *Are you looking for your mom?* I was worse, even, because I knew what had happened, and I'd messed up anyway.

"Well," I said. "I'm sitting with him for lunch, and with our friend Chloe Silver. You don't know her because she's new, and she's great. If you want to sit with us, you could. We'd really like you to."

Serena shifted her weight from one foot to the other, and her bowl of chili slid down her tray. I reached out so it wouldn't spill.

"Thanks," she said, and I wasn't sure if she was thanking me for the invitation or the spillage prevention. "I told Vanessa I'd sit with her."

"Okay. Well, if Vanessa wants to sit with us, she can, too."

"I think Vanessa promised Rachael we'd sit with her and her friends. But thanks for asking me."

We said good-bye. Serena walked over to the It Girls, and I walked back to the Kindness Club table. I didn't need to explain to Chloe and Theo what had happened, because of course they'd been watching, and even if they didn't hear the words that had been said, they'd been able to see the important parts: I'd asked Serena to sit with us, and she'd walked to the It Girls table instead. I felt majorly bummed out. There was still half a bowl of chili left on my plate, but I wasn't hungry anymore.

I twisted around in my seat to look at the It Girls. Serena's back was to me, so I couldn't see her face. But I could see Monroe. She had her hands up, gesturing vaguely in my direction as she spoke to the other girls. "It's like Monroe thinks she's the star of a show, and everyone else around is just her audience," I said.

"You could say that about each of our lives," Theo said. "I'm the star of *The Theo Show*, and Chloe is the star of *The*

Chloe Show." Chloe smiled and batted her eyes at him. "And you're the star of *The Lucy Show*. We're each other's audiences."

"I guess," I said. "But I still think Monroe is different from the rest of us. She thinks her show is the most important show in the world. She doesn't think about anyone else having shows of their own. And she certainly doesn't care about the audience that's watching her."

"I think she cares very much that people are watching her," Theo said. "She wants to make sure people are watching her all the time."

"I mean she doesn't care about what's going on in their lives," I said. "She doesn't care if she hurts their feelings while she's busy performing."

"Serena's a part of Monroe's audience," Chloe said.

"Yeah," I said. "So?"

"Soooooo," Chloe said, elongating the word, like it had three syllables instead of just one. "Monroe invited Serena to sit at her table."

"Actually I think Rachael did."

"Still, Monroe let her sit there, and she let Vanessa, too. They didn't used to be friends, so maybe it's because she feels bad for her, same as us. I'm not saying Monroe wants to plan a birthday party for her or anything that big, but she included her. That's kind, I think."

Chloe had me there. I didn't know what to say.

I looked at the It Girls table again. I couldn't help myself.

Whatever Monroe had said had made everyone else start laughing. Maybe it wasn't about me. Though I strongly suspected it was.

"Does this mean the party is off?" Theo asked.

"No, of course not," I said. "All this means is we don't get to talk to Serena beforehand, which maybe is better, because like you said, I wouldn't necessarily be crafty about getting the details out of her without her figuring out what was going on."

"So what do we do now?" Chloe asked. "Start inviting people?"

"Yeah."

"Who's on the guest list besides us and Vanessa?"

"I don't know," I admitted. "But we can make an estimate. I'll tell my dad to reserve three lanes, or even four to be safe. And we can conference call Vanessa tonight about the guest list. But what if she says we should invite the It Girls?"

"Then we invite them," Chloe said. "It's for Serena."

She was right, of course.

"Okay," I said. "We'll call Vanessa tonight."

"And before that," Chloe said, "I have a surprise for you guys." She grabbed the paper bag that she'd stashed on an empty chair. I'd totally forgotten about it. "Homemade pie," she said, pulling out a Tupperware container.

She peeled off the top, and I took a sniff. "Wow, thanks," I said.

"Yes, thank you," Theo said.

"Baked by me and my dad," Chloe said. "He's really into baking gluten-free things these days. He says it presents him with a new challenge."

"You're telling me this pie is gluten-free?" Theo asked.

"Sage has celiac disease," Chloe said.

"Yeah, I remember your saying something about that," Theo said. "But I generally like desserts that are baked with flour. I'm feeling pretty dubious about a flour-free piecrust."

"It smells really good," I said.

"I promise you it tastes even better," Chloe said. "Give it a try."

She served us each a piece. I was a little nervous as I moved the first bite to my mouth. I didn't want to hurt Chloe's feelings if I didn't like it. But then, I didn't want to have to eat it, either.

But there was nothing to worry about. The crust was the perfect mix of flaky and crunchy, and the apples were sweet and delicious. Theo and I each polished off a piece, and so did Chloe.

"There's so much left over," I said.

"Do you want another piece?"

"I do," I said. "But I'm actually pretty full from the first one."

"Good," she said. "I mean, I would've given you more. But I brought extra to give to Gwen and Fernando."

"Who are they?"

"The people who work in the cafeteria," she said. "Do you know they're also husband and wife."

"No," I said. "I didn't even know their names. How did you?"

"I asked them," she said. "They're really nice."

"When did you talk to them?"

"I had a question about how to cook quinoa, and I figured they'd know the answer, since they cook for five hundred kids every day."

"That's twenty-five hundred meals a week," Theo said.

"Yup," Chloe said. "And it's not like they're regular teachers who kids sometimes give holiday and end-of-year presents to. I wanted to do something nice for them."

Right then I felt a little embarrassed that I'd always taken Gwen and Fernando for granted. I'd never even wondered about their names. "I love how you remember to be kind to everyone," I told Chloe. "You do way more than three kind things a day, without even trying. I'm really glad you're my friend."

"I'm really glad you're mine, too. And you too, Theo. Want to come with me to bring them?"

Theo and I said yes. We cleaned up our food and headed over.

CHAPTER 16

Chloe, Theo, and I called Vanessa's house on Monday night, but Mrs. Medina said Vanessa was doing homework and unavailable to talk. We left a message but didn't hear back.

Now it was Tuesday. T-minus five days till Serena's birthday. Time was tick-tick-ticking away. We didn't have an invite list, but we figured maybe we could catch Vanessa during lunch. It would be difficult if she was sitting at the It Girls table again, to say nothing of how difficult it would be if she was with Serena. But maybe she'd break away on her own. We only needed to talk to her for a couple minutes, and we were crossing our fingers that she'd get up to get extra ketchup or some napkins, or maybe bring her tray over to the conveyor belt on her own, the way she had on Friday.

"It feels a little bit like we're stalking Vanessa," Chloe said uncomfortably. We were at our table, chairs slightly turned to watch her without being super obvious about the fact that we were watching her.

"Yeah, maybe I'll just call her again tonight," I said.

But then something completely unexpected happened.

It was Serena herself, approaching our table. She was balancing a tray of today's special: fish sticks and a side of fries, courtesy of Gwen and Fernando.

"Hi, Lucy," Serena said.

"Oh, hey," I said.

She nodded toward Theo. "Hi."

"Hi," he replied.

"Is everything okay?" I asked.

Serena's face scrunched up, like she didn't understand the question.

Or, more likely, she didn't know how to answer it. Of course she didn't, because of course everything wasn't okay. Her mom had died. And just like that, I'd brought up her mom again.

"Everything's fine," she said. "I was just wondering— could I sit with you guys today?"

"Yes, absolutely!" I said, a little too enthusiastically, and I took a deep, silent breath to calm down. "Sure you can."

"Thanks."

I was next to Chloe, and Serena walked around the table to sit on Theo's side.

"We haven't met yet," Chloe said. "I'm Chloe. I just moved here."

"Oh, I'm sorry," I broke in. "I'm so bad at introductions. Chloe, meet Serena. Serena, meet Chloe."

"Nice to meet you," Serena said.

"You too," Chloe told her. Then she added, "I was sorry to hear about your mom."

Oh, no! Now Chloe had brought her up, too!

"Thanks," Serena said softly.

She bent her head toward her plate, studying her fish sticks as if she was going to be tested on them later. I knew I needed to change the subject—stat!

"Just so you know," I said. "You can sit with us anytime you'd like. We're always at this table. We have a club of our own—the Kindness Club."

"Yeah, I heard about that," Serena said. "It sounds cool."

"It is," I said. "It's totally cool. And we have extra room, as you can see. We have room for Vanessa, if you think she'd want to sit here. Since you're here, she probably does. Oh, and if there's anyone else you think of, we can squeeze them in, too."

But Serena just shrugged. "I'm fine with just you guys," she said. "Vanessa is sitting at the It Girls' table again."

"Did you two have a fight?" Theo asked.

"No. Why would you think that?"

"Because every day the two of you are both in school, you sit together," Theo explained. "I've never seen you guys deviate from that pattern. When an anomaly occurs, it's usually because there's been a variant, and a disagreement would be a variant."

"Thank you, Dr. Barnes," Chloe said.

"She's my best friend and we don't fight," Serena said. She paused. "But you're right. There is a variant. The DML."

"I don't know what that is," I admitted.

"It's an acronym my aunt made up."

"Technically it's not an acronym if you don't pronounce the letters as a word," Theo told her.

I said the number-one word I always say in front of Theo: "Huh?"

"An acronym is an abbreviation formed by the first letters of other words, and pronounced as its own word," he explained. "For example, NASA and POTUS, which are the National Aeronautics and Space Administration, and the president of the United States, respectively."

And then I said the number-two word I always say in front of Theo, usually in response to one of his explanations that I only sort of understand. "Oh."

"If you can't pronounce it as a word, then it's just an initialism," he went on. "But don't feel bad. Most people don't know that. I'd bet a lot of teachers get it wrong, which means their students learn it wrong, and they grow up and tell other people the wrong definition. It's a vicious cycle."

"So what does DML mean?" I asked.

"The Dead Mother Look," Serena said. "I told my aunt everyone was looking at me funny since it happened. My aunt's mom died when she was younger. Like, older than we are. But still pretty young."

"That would be your dad's mom, too, then?" I asked.

Serena nodded. "And Odessa made up the acronym back then—I mean the *initials*. DML. It was a thing she said to herself in her head. I feel like I'm saying it all day long, because everyone gives it to me. Even Vanessa. She doesn't even know it. Even Mr. Dibble did. Yesterday, he told me to stop by his office during lunch to tell him how I was doing, and when I did, he gave me that look. And today Mr. Goldfarb asked a question and I raised my hand to answer. Before he called on me, he looked at me like that."

"Is it possible you're wrong?" Theo asked. "You know the way we perceive things isn't always accurate. Our brains constantly try to correct images so that we see them the way we expect to see them."

"Like seeing water in a desert when it's not really there?" Chloe asked.

"No, that's a mirage, which has to do with the speed that light travels through cold and hot air. This is different. It's your brain trying to make things easier on you." He turned back to Serena. "I'm just saying, if you were expecting to see people looking at you a certain way, well then, maybe you saw something that wasn't actually happening."

"It's not just a trick my brain was playing, I swear," Serena said. "Mr. Goldfarb had been asking questions all morning, and he called on a bunch of people. But when he saw my hand raised, he tilted his head, like one of his ears was suddenly heavier. His eyes got squinty. And he waited a couple seconds before he said, 'Yes, Serena?' That's the DML, and whenever I see it, which is all the time, it makes me feel even worse about what happened."

I checked myself to make sure I was holding my head straight as Serena kept talking. I thought it was, but maybe that was one of Theo's brain tricks: I perceived my head as straight even though it really wasn't.

"And there's something else. Something even worse."

"What?" I asked.

"I think people want to be my friend because this happened. The It Girls never cared about Vanessa and me before. Now we're allowed to sit at their table."

"Maybe they didn't realize they wanted to be friends with you till now," Chloe said. "Like I didn't know you before now, but I'm happy we met."

"Thanks," Serena said. "But I don't want to be more popular because my mom died. That's not . . ." Her voice dropped. "That's not fair to her."

"I think your mom would want you to be happy," Chloe said, her own voice dropped to match Serena's soft tone.

"Yeah, that's what everyone says," Serena said. "But how would they know? It's not like she told them."

"She told my mom," Theo said. "I overheard my mom tell my dad that she said it. She was worried about you. She wanted you to be happy."

Serena nodded. "Okay, then."

"Anyway, you don't have to worry about it with us," I told her. "We're not popular."

Serena gave me the tiniest of tiny smiles.

"So that's why you didn't want to sit at their table," Theo said.

"Partly," Serena replied. "But mostly because of the DML. They do it as bad as anyone."

"I just want you to know," Chloe said, "if I give you a look like that, it's totally by accident. I *do* feel sorry that your mom died, but I don't want to make you upset."

"I don't, either," I said. "That isn't why I invited you to lunch. You know that, right?"

"She's here, isn't she?" Theo asked.

"Yeah, but you heard what she just said."

"It's okay," Serena said. "I didn't mind with you."

"You mean, because my mom also died?"

"Yeah," Serena said. "I'm sorry. I never thought about how hard it must be until it happened to me."

"Don't worry about it," I told her, feeling that tingle I always felt when I was reminded that I didn't have a mom. "It was a long time ago."

Serena didn't say anything back, and neither did Theo or Chloe. I picked up a fish stick, took a bite, and put it back down. All around, there were the regular lunch sounds happening, people talking, chairs scraping, trays being picked up and put down. Parallel lives, like Mrs. G said.

"Hey, I have a game we should play," I said. "It's called Word Association. Ollie made it up one day when he was babysitting and I was bored."

"He didn't make it up," Theo said. "It's a relatively common game."

"Well, I'd never played it before until he played it with me," I said. "And I'll tell you how it works. I say a word, and then you say back whatever you think of. Serena first. What's your favorite color?"

"Green," she said.

"Favorite song?"

"Hang on," Theo interrupted. "This isn't how you play word association."

"I'm doing it my way," I told Theo. "You know I'm a crafty girl."

"Super crafty," Chloe agreed.

"Yeah, I guess you are," Theo said. "Carry on."

"Thanks," I said. "So, Serena, favorite singer?"

"Taylor Swift," she said.

"Favorite cake flavor?"

"Chocolate."

"Oh, good choice. Mine too. Now . . . what about hot dogs versus hamburgers—which do you prefer?"

"I don't eat meat," she said.

"No meat," I said, committing that to memory. "I'm glad I asked."

"Why?" she asked.

"Oh, no reason. It's just—whether or not someone is a vegetarian is something you should know about your friends."

"I'm not a vegetarian," Serena said. "I'm a pescatarian. I eat fish."

"Clearly," Theo said. "She's eating fish sticks."

"Yeah, but I'm done now."

Serena had barely had more than half a stick and a couple fries, but she balled up her napkin and put it atop her plate.

"Who are your friends in Mr. Goldfarb's class?" I asked her. "I mean, besides Vanessa?"

"Katie Hartman and Kai Williams," she said. "And Kris Polakov, too."

"So anyone whose name starts with a *K*," Chloe said.

"Oh, yeah," Serena said. "I never noticed that, but I think they're the only *K* names in class and I'm friends with them all."

"I'm glad there's a boy in there," Theo said. "I'm always surrounded by girls."

"Why does it matter?" Serena asked. "He's not at this table."

"And you love being surrounded by girls," I said quickly. Theo had almost blown our cover. Then again, I'd almost blown our cover a couple times, too. "Anyway, let's keep playing," I said.

"Actually, I should probably go," Serena said. "Mr. Dibble wants me to stop by his office again. He said I should eat first and it'd be okay if I was late to class after, but I don't want to be late. Everyone will look at me if I walk in late."

She scraped her chair back and lifted her tray. "But would it be okay if I sit with you guys again tomorrow?"

"Yes, of course," Theo said.

I grinned. "Absolutely."

CHAPTER 17

Vanessa caught up with us at the end of lunch, when Chloe, Theo, and I were bringing our trays over to the conveyor belt. "Hey," she said. "Do you know where Serena went?"

"To Mr. Dibble's office."

"She saw him yesterday."

"She said he wanted her to stop by again today."

"Oh," Vanessa said.

It was weird to know information about Serena that Vanessa didn't have. I think we both felt awkward about it. I stepped back so she could drop her tray on the conveyor belt. "So, Vanessa," I said. "There's something else I wanted to tell you. I—well, *we*, meaning Chloe, Theo, and me. Have you met Chloe, by the way?"

"No, not yet."

"Vanessa, this is Chloe. Chloe, this is Vanessa."

They said hi to each other, and I was about to tell Vanessa

the next part—about the party we were organizing for Serena, but I didn't get a chance because then came Monroe Reeser. She was carrying a tray of her own, but she made no move to place it on the conveyor belt. Instead, she balanced it on one hand, and put her other hand on her hip.

It occurred to me that there are certain kids who can do that, hold a tray in one hand; and there are other kids whose trays would topple over if they tried. But Monroe is not the kind of person whose tray ever topples over. It's like even gravity is afraid to mess with her.

"I know you're in the business of stealing friends, Lucy," she said to me, and her eyes flashed to Chloe for an instant. "But don't even try to steal Serena from Vanessa."

"I wasn't stealing her!" I said.

"She couldn't if she wanted to," Theo said. "Serena doesn't belong to Vanessa. People don't belong to other people. Unless you're talking about parents and kids, and then, from a purely custodial standpoint, I suppose they do. But even parents can't control who their kids want to be friends with. There are a lot of factors that go into it, and only one of them is familial acceptance."

"I didn't ask for your opinion," Monroe told him. "Don't let us catch you talking to Serena again."

Serena had asked if she could sit with us again tomorrow, and I wasn't going to let Monroe bully me into not letting her. "But—" I started.

"It's okay," Vanessa said. "Theo's right. Serena is allowed

to be friends with whoever she wants to be friends with. I don't own her."

She looked so sad, almost as sad as Serena had looked at lunch, and I knew I needed to say something to make her feel better. "She's still your friend," I said. "She's still your best friend. She even called you her best friend when we were talking at lunch."

"Really?"

"Yeah. In fact, I'm glad you caught me because there's something about Serena we need to talk to you about. We called you last night."

"My mom said someone called. She didn't write down the name, though. It was you?"

"It was all of us," I said. I could feel Monroe watching me, waiting to hear what I was about to say. I didn't want to talk about Serena's party in front of her, because then she'd be on the invite list. But I didn't think there was any way to avoid it. "We're planning a party for her—for her birthday."

Jesse Freeman stepped over with his tray. "Excuse me, guys," he said. "You're sort of blocking things here."

"Sorry," Chloe said.

The group of us shuffled to the side of the conveyor belt. "Ah, so that's why she wanted to sit with you," Monroe said to me. "Because you were bribing her."

"No," I said. "Serena doesn't even know about it. It's a total surprise."

"I'm not sure if she wants a party," Vanessa said. "Birthdays were kind of her mom's thing."

"I spoke to her aunt the other day."

"You talked to Odessa."

"Mmm hmm," I said. "And she thought a party was a great idea. She was happy we were doing it. And at lunch today, we got a little bit of information out of Serena. Just details to make it the kind of party she'd want, like her favorite color for the balloons."

"Green," Vanessa said. "She likes green."

"Yup, and she said chocolate is her favorite cake flavor."

"With vanilla icing," Vanessa said.

"Oh, good to know. Also she said she doesn't eat meat, but do you know if she likes pizza? Or is there any other food we should have?"

"She likes pizza," Vanessa said. "Pizza would be good."

"Cool."

"I know Serena is friends with Kai, Katie, and Kris from your class. Is there anyone else, you think?"

"Well, Rachael, obviously," Vanessa said. "And Monroe and Anjali from your class, of course."

"O-kay," I said slowly. "If they want to come."

"We'll be there," Monroe said.

"So with the three of us, and Serena's dad and aunt, that makes . . ." I started ticking names off my fingers, but I didn't have enough fingers and I lost count.

"Thirteen people," Theo said.

"Plus she has two brothers," Vanessa said.

"Fifteen," Theo said, not that I needed him to do the math on that one.

"Great," Chloe said.

"Uh-oh," I said.

"What?"

"Theo wanted the invite list to be a multiple of four so the number of bowlers on each lane would match up. We need one more."

"We can invite Eleanor Barrett, but then we have to invite Bea Johnson, and neither of them is so close with Serena anyway," Vanessa said.

"I'll invite my mom," Theo said. "She knows Serena."

"Perfect. Sixteen. Four lanes." I turned to Vanessa. "Does that sound good?"

"It sounds great," she said.

"There's just one more thing," I said.

"What's that?"

I knew what I was about to say would be awkward, but I figured that I should say it anyway. It was the kind thing to do—for Serena. "She doesn't want people looking at her like they feel sorry for her."

"Of course we feel sorry," Monroe said, with a roll of her eyes. "Her mother died. And that's how people feel when that happens."

"I think Lucy would know that better than any of us," Chloe said.

For once, Monroe was quiet. There was nothing for her to say: My mom was dead. That was a fact. Tingles again.

"She knows people feel bad," I said softly. I turned to Theo. "Or do I mean badly?"

He shook his head. "You had it right the first time."

"People feel bad," I said. "But it's hard for Serena when they look at her like she's different now."

"She said I looked at her like that?" Vanessa asked.

I nodded. "She did. She wasn't mad or anything. I don't think she thought you were doing it on purpose."

"I wasn't. But I'll try not to do it again."

"Cool," I said. "Can you help us spread the word to everyone on the guest list?"

"Of course."

The five-minute bell rang. "I guess that means we should get going," I said.

"Yeah, I guess it does," Vanessa said.

"Come on," Monroe told her. "Rachael and Anjali are waiting for us."

"Okay," she said. "And Lucy?"

"Yeah?"

"I want to help with this. I'm her best friend, so if there's a party I should help plan it. If you guys think of anything else you need, will you let me know?"

I nodded. "We definitely will," I told her.

CHAPTER 18

Once again, Dad was at Tanaka Lanes super late on Tuesday evening, which meant he missed dinner with Grandma and me. And that was too bad for him, because Grandma made one of my very favorite things, something I've only eaten at my house maybe twice in my whole life: a box of Kraft macaroni and cheese.

"I'm glad you're enjoying your pasta, mago," Grandma said. "But the nutritional value lies solely in the side dish." She nodded toward the broccoli on a small plate next to my big mac-and-cheese bowl.

I finished my mouthful of cheesy deliciousness and speared a piece of broccoli to make her happy. Then I went back to eating the Kraft. "So Dad's really busy still, huh?" I asked.

"He is," she said.

"Just with regular work stuff?"

"Yes."

"You're sure it's not something else?"

"You worry too much," she said. "You always have."

"No, I don't." I rested my fork at the edge of my plate. "But if I don't worry, how can I try to make things okay?"

"Things have a way of working themselves out," Grandma said.

"Well, the details of this party won't get worked out on their own."

"What party is that?"

"The one we're having for Serena at the bowling alley on Sunday."

"Serena's family is throwing her a party?" Grandma asked.

"No. *We* are. The Kindness Club."

"Oh, mago, I don't know if your dad can swing that right now."

"He already told me it was okay," I said.

"He did? When?"

"At breakfast last Friday," I told her. "You were there. Don't tell me you forgot."

"I'm sorry, mago," Grandma said. "I don't recall him saying that."

"Well, he did," I said. "And now I'm worried about you again. You've forgotten a bunch of things lately. We were sitting right there, eating scrambled eggs. Only Dad was standing, and he wasn't eating eggs because he said he wasn't hungry. You said you'd package some up for him to bring to work. Then he got mad at me because I wanted him to have a fresh breakfast."

"I remember that part," she said.

"Okay," I said. "Good. So now I really need to talk to him. Maybe I should call him."

"Let him work," Grandma said. "You can speak to him later."

"Okay."

We finished up dinner and cleaned all the dishes. Grandma put the leftovers for Dad in the fridge. I didn't tell Grandma this, but I knew Dad would also be secretly happy about what was on the menu. Not that we didn't love Grandma's cooking. But Ollie, Dad, and I all loved Kraft mac and cheese, too.

Later on, I went up to my room. Dad still wasn't back. It was getting late, but I wanted to talk to him before I went to sleep so I could plan my dream out better: What would the perfect party for Serena look like? In the meantime, I finished my homework and reread a bunch of old fashion magazines. I hadn't begun to think about what I'd wear on Sunday. It had to be something birthday appropriate and also bowling appropriate.

In my family, we're all pretty serious about our bowling. Lots of kids bowl with bumpers in the lanes. That means there's something blocking the gutters, so as long as you swing your arm hard enough, your ball will roll down the middle and knock down at least a few pins. There's absolutely nothing wrong with using bumpers. But Dad spent a lot time teaching Ollie and me to bowl so we wouldn't need them.

When I was little, I held the ball with both hands, because it was heavy and my fingers were too small for the holes. But now that I'm ten I have my own ball that my fingers actually fit into—my thumb and my first two fingers. A perfect grip. The better to knock the pins down.

There are ten pins in a bowling lane. For each turn, a bowler gets two shots at rolling their ball at the pins. If you knock them all down at once, that's a strike, and that's really hard to do. If it takes you two turns to knock them down, that's called a spare, and that's also hard but not as hard.

Over the years, I've learned a lot about bowling. Mostly from Dad and Grandma, but some from Ollie, too, and even from Felix. He was a really patient bowling teacher. Before he left Dad in the lurch, I thought he was so kind. But it turned out he wasn't.

I lay back on my bed and closed my eyes to see the vision board of Serena's party inside my head. I decided to wear my lucky bowling pants, along with the olive green shirt that I'd gotten last month at Second Chance. I hadn't worn it yet because the sleeves were too long and the cuffs were too tight, and I hadn't figured out how I wanted to fix them. Plus, it was just too plain. But I could make it one of my "scenes" shirts—the scene from a bowling alley, and I'd pair it with my forest green leggings and silver bowling shoes.

I must've fallen asleep thinking about it. When my alarm rang Wednesday morning, the light in my room had been turned off, and the magazines were closed up and placed neatly on my dresser. By the time I got downstairs for breakfast, Dad had already left for work—again. "Mrs. G says things always change," I told Grandma. "I can't wait till it changes back to Dad being less busy so I actually see him again."

"That's sweet that you miss him."

"I do, and now it's only four days away and we haven't discussed any party details. He doesn't even know how many lanes to reserve."

"You need more than one lane?" Grandma asked.

"We need four," I told her.

"Four?"

"There are sixteen people on the guest list," I explained. "We need to talk about the menu, too. Serena likes pizza, but no meat toppings because she's a pescatarian. And she likes chocolate cake with white icing. I think Chloe can take care of that, because she's a great baker. But the alley will have to supply the balloons—green ones. I'll write it all down for you to give to Dad. Do you think he could put green spotlights on the lanes? Do you think green balloons and green lights is too much of one color?"

"I don't know, mago," Grandma said.

"Well, I think it's too much," I said. "Even when you love

a color, sometimes you can have too much of it. So maybe the balloons can be green and the lights can be another color, like pink. Green and pink look good together. Though I'm not sure if Serena is a pink kind of girl."

"I meant I'm not sure if Dad can do the lights for you," Grandma said.

"He's done colored lights before," I reminded her. "Remember Disco Night?"

"Mmm hmm."

"Maybe I should just call him so you don't need to remember everything."

"You said you were going to write it down," Grandma said.

"Yeah," I said. "But."

"But what? You don't trust me to deliver a note?"

"Of course I trust you," I told her. "It's just—this is important to me. It's important to our club, and to Serena. What if you forget?"

Grandma shook her head. "I'll talk to your father. Are you done with that?"

She nodded toward my plate. Only the crust of my cinnamon toast remained. "Yeah, I'm done," I said.

I stood to throw out the scraps and rinse my plate, but Grandma took it from me. "I've got this," she said. "You should pack up what you need for school and get going. And after school—"

"I know, I know," I said. "After school I go to Mrs. Negishi's. She's going to be mad that I haven't practiced these last couple weeks. But it's not really my fault because last week she canceled, and this week I've been busy with the club, and—"

"Lucy—" Grandma cut in.

"Oh, hey," I said. "Can you write me a note? I've seen kids bring notes to teachers when they haven't done their homework and they have a good excuse. If it works in school, then it should definitely work for an after-school piano lesson. Don't you think?"

"You don't need one," she said.

"You don't know Mrs. Negishi," I told her.

"I do in fact know Mrs. Negishi. But you don't have piano this afternoon."

"Again?" I asked. "Is she still away?"

"No, she's back. But you told me you didn't like the lessons, so I told Mrs. Negishi we weren't signing up again."

"Oh," I said.

"You're disappointed?" Grandma asked.

"No," I said. I thought back to what Grandma has said about insisting I take piano lessons in the first place: because learning the piano wasn't just about piano—it was also about concentration and coordination. "I'm just surprised, that's all." The doorbell rang. "That's Theo," I said.

"Go on, Lucy," Grandma said. "You don't want to keep him waiting."

CHAPTER 19

Serena sat with Chloe, Theo, and me again during lunch. It was hard to contain our excitement about the party, but the three of us managed to act mostly normal. Except for one moment, when I looked over at the It Girls' table, where Vanessa was. We caught each other's eye, and I gave a secret little wave.

"Hey, Lucy," Chloe said. "Are we going back to the Community House tomorrow to give the kids the quilt?"

"Oh, yeah," I said. "Absolutely."

"What kids?" Serena asked. "What quilt?"

"We volunteered at the after-school program last week," I explained.

"For your kind club?"

"Yup. And we brought supplies for the kids to each decorate a square of fabric."

"Or a rectangle, or a heart shape," Chloe said.

"All different shapes," I said. "I sewed them together to make a patchwork quilt. It wasn't as easy as I thought it would be, but it came out all right. Not perfect, but all right."

"That's so cool," Serena said.

"You can come with us to give it to them, if you want."

"Oh, I wish," Serena said. "I have to go to the orthodontist. I was supposed to go already, but my mom was really sick when I had the appointment, so we had to reschedule."

Every time Serena mentioned her mom, I felt something tighten inside me. Like the tingles for my mom, and something even more. Almost like I missed Mrs. Kappas, which didn't even make sense because I'd never met her.

Or maybe I did meet her. It was possible that she once stood next to Grandma at after-school pickup, when we were too young to walk home by ourselves. Or maybe she was one of the parents who volunteered at the annual carnival night, and she handed me a prize or an ice cream cone. I couldn't remember. I'd had language during those times, but I didn't know some things were important enough to store as memories.

"I'd like to skip it again," Serena went on. "But my aunt thinks we've put off the orthodontist long enough, and I know she won't let me out of it."

"Do you go to Dr. Beach?" Chloe asked her. "He's my orthodontist, and he's not so bad."

"I don't know," Serena said. "It's my first time."

"Ooh," Chloe said. "I hope it's Dr. Beach. He has a big

whiteboard in his waiting room that takes up the whole back wall and you can draw whatever you want. Some people even write jokes or poems on it."

"What did you put on it?" Serena asked.

"Serotonin," Chloe said.

"Sero-what?"

"It's the chemical in your brain that makes you happier," Theo explained.

"It looks like two hexagons put together with some lines coming out of the sides. I drew it on the bottom right corner. It might still be there. Dr. Beach doesn't erase anything until the board is completely covered, and then it starts over."

Our class has science the last two periods on Wednesday, and right in the middle of the lesson about the three different types of matter, I had another idea. Chloe, Theo, and I all sit in a row, but I couldn't risk passing a note. Our science teacher, Dr. Whelan, is super strict. If you so much as smile at the person next to you, she yells at you for not paying attention. I've seen her do it to other people and it's humiliating. So I waited for the bell to ring, and then I told my fellow Kindness Club members my plan: "I'm going to go to Tanaka Lanes right now and make sure everything is all set for Sunday."

"I thought your piano teacher was back this week," Chloe said.

"She is," I said. "But my grandmother said I don't have to go anymore."

"Then I'll go with you," Chloe said. "If you want me to."

"I definitely want you to," I said. "But don't you have to finish your homework before you go to your dad's?"

"It's not like that's a rule," she said. "He just likes me to try and get everything done. But I think he'd understand if I do this instead. After all, the Kindness Club started out as a school project. And besides that, I haven't even ever seen Tanaka Lanes."

"That is a complete and total tragedy that we need to fix IMMEDIATELY," I said.

Theo said he'd come, too—he didn't want to miss Chloe's first time at the alley. The three of us headed down Braywood School Road, made a left on Main, and a right onto Sheridan.

I love turning the corner and seeing the sign for Tanaka Lanes. It's on a pole that stretches up high, like twenty feet aboveground at least. TANAKA LANES is spelled out in big, bold letters, and next to them there's a picture of a couple pins and a bowling ball. At night the sign lights up and the letters flash off and on in neon blue. During the day, the lights are off. But still, it's pretty big and it looks cool.

We crossed the street and ran along the sidewalk to the thick glass double doors. I pulled one open. "After you," I said to my friends.

"Finally, FINALLY, I'm at the famous Tanaka Lanes," Chloe said.

"It is kind of famous," I agreed. "Everyone in town knows about it. Come on, I'll show you everything."

But we barely made it more than five feet inside before someone stopped us. "Excuse me," a woman said. I'd never seen her before. She was sitting behind the desk where you sign up for your lane and get your shoes. "Children under sixteen are not allowed to be in here without a parent. Is your mother with you?"

Different adult, same assumption.

"My *father* is with me," I said. "I'm Lucy." I looked at her eyes for a sign of recognition on hearing my name. But: nothing. "Lucy *Tanaka*. My dad is Kenji Tanaka, and he owns this place. We're going to go to his office." I turned to Chloe. "Which is right up there," I said, pointing to a staircase that at first glance she probably hadn't seen. The lights are dimmed at Tanaka Lanes, like it's always nighttime inside the bowling alley, and the stairs leading up to Dad's office are carpeted in black, so people don't usually notice them. Upstairs, there are one-way windows. Dad can see out, onto the lanes. But if you're on the first floor looking up, you'd only see the lanes reflected back to you in mirrors.

"Why don't you wait right here and I'll call for him," the woman told me.

"I'm allowed to go up without calling," I assured her.

She shook her head. "Wait here."

She picked up the phone, and I listened to her half of the conversation: "Hi, this is Lydia from downstairs. I have some visitors for Ken?" She said it like it was a question. "His daughter and a couple other kids?" Another question. There was a brief pause, someone else talking. Then Lydia said, "All right. I will."

"He said to come up?" I asked as she hung up the phone.

"Someone will be right with you," she said.

"Okay," I said.

"May I use the phone?" Chloe asked.

"We don't usually allow customers to use the phone," Lydia said.

"She's not a customer," I told her. "She's my guest."

"It'll only be a minute," Chloe said. "I just need to call my mom and let her know where I am."

Lydia slid the phone toward Chloe. I listened to her tell her mom where she was. When she hung up, Theo called his parents. Then we sat in the waiting area, just, well, waiting. To be honest, it was a little boring, and I felt bad. This was Chloe's first time at Tanaka Lanes! It should be the opposite of boring!

"Hey!" I said. "You guys, let's bowl!"

We needed to go to Lydia for shoes, which she didn't want to give us. But I knew where everything was, so I grabbed three pair for Chloe, Theo, and myself—I hadn't brought my bowling shoes with me, so I had to use a communal pair. Kind of gross. Lydia picked up the phone again, I bet to call up to Dad's office and check that I was really allowed to do what I said. Meanwhile, I led my friends toward the bowling lanes. First we each had to pick a bowling ball.

"You want a ball where your fingers fit firmly, but they don't stick when you're trying to get them out," I advised.

Chloe picked up a pink ball. "This one's good, and it's really light."

"It's too light," I told her. "You need it to be light enough to swing around, but also heavy enough to knock the pins with force. It's a little like having the perfect handshake: there's a balance."

"It's physics," Theo said. "The mass of the ball affects how fast it travels down the lane."

Chloe nodded, though I could tell she didn't really understand. Neither did I. But I did know about picking bowling balls. I handed Chloe a yellow one and took green for myself. Theo picked an orange one.

"Oh, by the way, they glow in the dark," I said. "Wait till you see how cool it looks rolling down the lane."

It was a Wednesday afternoon, not exactly prime bowling time, so there were lots of lanes to choose from. I picked Lane 3. There's a little computer in front of each lane, where you can type in your names to go up on the screen, so you know whose turn it is. Ollie always made up cool bowling names, so I did that, too:

Chloe the Kindest
Theo Barnestormer
Lucky Lucy

"I put you first because you've never been here before, so you're the guest of honor," I told Chloe. "Do you want any pointers?"

"Sure."

"Okay. These are the four main things Felix taught me. Number one, keep your wrist strong, so the ball is like an extension of your arm. Number two, there are marks on the lane and you should find your mark and that's what you aim for when you swing the ball. Number three, use a four-step approach to your swing: step, step, step, step, pulling your arm back and forward again. Finally, number four, release the ball on your fourth step, keeping your hand straight and palm up the whole time."

Chloe nodded and picked up her ball. I watched her eye the marks, then she counted her steps: "One, two, three, four." When she released it, it rolled down the center for a couple seconds, before veering left. "Oh no! Gutter ball!"

"It's okay, you'll get the hang of it," I assured her.

Each bowler gets two turns, so when Chloe's ball popped back up, she tried again and knocked a couple pins down. Then it was Theo's turn. He got four pins down his first shot, and one the next. "You're up, Lucky Lucy."

I picked up my green ball and counted my steps, aiming for the second mark on the right. That was my mark. Felix had told me after watching me bowl like a thousand times. One. Two. Three. Four. Swing and release. At first it looked like the ball was going to hit the right-side pins only. But it smashed the pins exactly in the center of the lane. Crash. They all went down. An instant replay flashed on the score screen above our heads.

Chloe ran up and slapped me five. "That was amazing," she said.

"Thanks."

"Do you always get strikes?" Theo asked.

I shook my head. "I'm pretty good at getting pins down, but usually I don't get strikes. My brother gets them all the time, though. Did you know when you get three strikes in a row, it's called a turkey, and when that happens, a cartoon turkey appears up there." I nodded toward the screen.

"What's it called if you bowl four strikes in a row?"

"There isn't a name for it. People just say four-bagger, or five-bagger for five, and on and on. I need a turkey first, though."

"This could be your Lucky Lucy day," Chloe told me.

"Or yours," I told her. "You're up again."

"LUCY!" a voice called out—Grandma's voice.

"Hey! Grandma! I bowled a strike! Right on my first try. Maybe today will be a turkey day!"

"Or even a four-bagger," Chloe said. "Hello, Mrs. Tanaka."

"Hello, dear," Grandma said. She turned to me. "Is everything all right?"

"Yeah," I said. "We just came to check things out for Serena's party, and we decided to bowl while we waited for you and Dad. Is he done with his meeting?"

"He's finishing a call," Grandma told me. "He'll be down in a few minutes."

"I guess we'll keep bowling till then. Turkey, here I come!"

Grandma stepped toward the computer. "I don't think it's a good time for a game right now."

She pressed the button marked: *End Game.* "Okay," I said. "Well, can I show Chloe the back?"

It's really cool to see behind the scenes at Tanaka Lanes, where the pinsetters are. Everything runs like clockwork back there; except sometimes, there's a jam in the bowling ball machine. Then you have to unjam the balls by hand. But Dad never lets me do it, because the balls can smash your fingers.

Grandma shook her head. "Let's wait for Dad by the concession stand," she said.

"Can I make them Tanaka dogs?"

"He'll be down soon," she said.

But he wasn't down that soon. Certainly we could've eaten a Tanaka dog, and maybe two, before the office door finally opened and Dad padded down the dark stairwell. "Hey, Lucy," he said. "It's not a great day to be here. Grandma and I have a lot of work to do."

"Don't worry," I said. "We're not staying long. You remember Theo, right? And this is Chloe."

He looked at my friends like he was noticing them for the first time. "Yes, of course. Hi, Theo. Hi, Chloe."

They both said hi back to him. Then Chloe said, "It's really nice to meet you, Mr. Tanaka. I love your bowling alley."

"What?" Dad said. "Oh, thanks."

"We just came because we wanted to make sure everything was set for Sunday," I told him.

"Sunday?" Dad asked.

"Lucy says you agreed to host a party for her friend Serena," Grandma prompted.

"You *did* agree," I said. "Last week. I told you about how Serena's mom died and we were going to plan a birthday party for her. And now it's not just any party. It's a surprise party."

"Oh, Luce—" he began.

"Don't worry," I said. "I already spoke to Serena's aunt Odessa, and she said it's fine. She said it's great actually. She's going to bring her by at noon, and Serena's best friend Vanessa is telling all of Serena's friends about it. We're expecting sixteen people total, so we need four lanes, and we'll serve pizza because Serena's a vegetarian."

"Pescatarian," Theo broke in.

"Right, and—"

"Lucy, I need to stop you there," Dad said. His eyes flicked to my friends for an instant, then back to me. "I'm very sorry, but you can't have a party here this weekend."

"But, Dad," I said. "You promised."

"I'm pretty sure I didn't say that I promised anything."

"Okay, fine," I said. "You didn't specifically say the words 'I promise,' but you did say that the party was a good idea. I thought that meant we were allowed to go ahead with it."

"It's a misunderstanding," Dad said. "We can't."

"We have to!" I cried. "Serena's mom just died, and we're the Kindness Club! It's up to us to make her birthday special!"

"I'm sure Serena's family can handle that," he said.

"They can't! Dad, please!"

He shook his head.

I knew Chloe and Theo were right there, watching my dad, and watching me. I was so humiliated. This was even worse than if Dr. Whelan had yelled at me in front of the whole class. Even if Dad hadn't made a promise, *I'd* made one. And now he was making me break it. My stomach clenched, and I could feel pressure behind my eyes. The kind of pressure that means tears are coming.

"Please," I said again. My voice had that about-to-cry sound to it, too.

"I would if I could," Dad said.

"Now, come on, Lucy," Grandma said. "Calm down and don't give your father a hard time about this. I told you last night I wasn't sure it would work, and now he's said no."

"But he just said he would if he could and he *can*," I insisted. I turned to Dad. "Come on, you're the boss. You own this place. How can you be so unkind?"

"All right, that's enough," Dad said sharply. "We'll discuss this at home."

"Yeah, right," I muttered. "You're never home."

"What's that?"

The phone on Lydia's desk rang, and she picked it up. "Hello?" And a few seconds later, she looked over at us. "Ken, there's a call for you," she said.

"I'll take it upstairs," he told her, and he turned to head back up the black staircase.

"Why don't you go home now," Grandma said. "We'll talk about this later."

"Can you try to talk him into it?"

"No, Lucy," she said. "Your dad gave you an answer, and just because you don't like it doesn't mean I can change it." She glanced at Chloe and Theo, then back to me. "I think you three should try to think of a new plan."

CHAPTER 20

On the walk home, Theo and Chloe did their best to cheer me up and make me not feel bad about what happened. But of course I felt bad. I'd let them down. Worse still, I'd let Serena down.

Maybe that was Dad's fault, but it felt like it was my fault. Grandma said she didn't remember the discussion of the party, and Dad didn't seem to, either. So maybe it wasn't that the two of them were forgetting things; it was that I was making things up.

Except I was sure that I wasn't making it up. We had talked about it, and he had said it was okay. I played snippets of the conversation with Dad over in my head, like a memory movie:

"We have had some nice memories at the bowling alley, haven't we?"

"I think Serena would like a party there. Don't you think?"

"Yes, sure."

Meanwhile, Chloe and Theo debated whose house we should move the party to. The problem with Theo's house, he explained, was that his sister Anabelle was already hosting a party for the track team. It was the coach's birthday, too. The same day as Serena's. "Quite a coincidence, huh?" Chloe asked, elbowing me. She was smiling in a way that was supposed to make me smile, too. "What were the chances? Two out of twenty-three, according to Theo's birthday problem, right?"

"Fifty percent, if there are twenty-three people in the room," Theo corrected.

"Well, anyway," Chloe went on. "It's nothing to worry about. We'll just have Serena's party at my house."

"Your mom might say no," I said. To be honest, part of me hoped that she would. Then I wouldn't be the only person with a parent who wouldn't have a party for Serena. I knew that thought made me an unkind person, but I couldn't help it.

"I'm sure she'll say yes," Chloe said.

And she was right. When we got to her house, Chloe called Mrs. Silver and explained the situation.

"Thanks, Mom," Chloe said. She gave Theo and me the thumbs-up sign, and when she hung up, she turned to us and said, "We're all set!"

"That's great news," Theo said. "We can still decorate and make things look festive."

"Definitely," Chloe said. "But not right now. My mom wants me to do my homework before she gets home to take me to my dad's."

"That's fine," Theo said. "I have an experiment set up in my basement, and I need to move the grass under the blue light to under the red light."

"Lucy, do you want to stay?" Chloe asked. "We could do homework together."

I shook my head. "I better get home, too." Not because I had an experiment in the basement, and not because anyone wanted me home. I just wanted to be by myself for a while.

I walked down the block with Theo, toward both of our houses. He lives two blocks away from Chloe, and I live three. For the first block, we didn't talk at all. That was something good about Theo I'd never realized before—when you're in the mood for things to be quiet, it's easy to keep things that way, because most of the time he's happy just thinking things in his head. I was thinking things in my head, too. Things I didn't want to say out loud. Things I didn't even want to have to think about.

"Hey," Theo said suddenly. "I just realized we should've called Vanessa to tell her to spread the word about the change of venue. We can call together, if you want."

"Don't you have work to do?" I asked.

"Yeah, but if you want some company, that's okay, too."

I shook my head. "No, thanks," I said. "Would you mind calling Vanessa without me?"

"I don't mind," he said. We were quiet again for another half block. I could see Theo's house from where we were. With the sign staked in the yard, it was hard to miss:

THE BARNES CLINIC

STEPHEN BARNES, DVM

"I know you're upset," Theo said. "But it's not your fault. You know that, right?"

"It is," I said. "It's so dumb that I made my name 'Lucky Lucy' when we bowled. I'm actually the opposite. I'm letting everyone down. That means I don't have any luck at all."

"You only feel that way because of what happened to you."

"You'd feel that way, too, if your dad said you could have a party and then he unsaid it."

"I don't mean what happened at the alley," Theo said. "I mean what happened when you were little, with your mom. Kids whose moms die have more sadness and more fears, because they're missing someone who mattered so much."

Tingles.

So. Many. Tingles. From the tippy-top of my head to the tips of my toes.

"Did you read that in one of your textbooks?" I managed to ask.

"No," Theo said. "I heard my parents talking about it last night."

"Well, I think they're wrong. This isn't about my mom. I wasn't even thinking about her. I was thinking about Serena and her mom. I feel really bad . . . badly . . . whatever."

"Bad," Theo said. "Do you need me to do something kind for you right now to get your serotonin levels up? I have some of Anabelle's candy left. You could have some."

I shook my head. "I just want to go home."

"I'll see you tomorrow morning, Lucy," Theo said.

"Yup. See you."

CHAPTER 21

Dad didn't come home for dinner that night. Grandma said it was because he wanted to put a little space between us.

"You mean he's avoiding me?" I asked. As far as I knew, no one in my family had ever had a reason to avoid me before.

"He just needs a break today," Grandma said. She just stood and brought her bowl to the sink. I noticed she'd left most of her beef stew uneaten. So had I. I set my spoon down in the bowl with a soft *clink*. "You done?"

"Yeah."

She picked up my bowl. For the first time since the dishwasher had broken, I didn't offer to help her clean everything up.

"I have homework," I said.

"Well, go on then," Grandma said.

"Okay."

I was halfway out the door when she called me back. "Oh, hey, Lucy?"

"Yeah."

"I spoke to Valerie at the Community House. She said she thought you were coming in again."

"Right. I promised the kids I'd bring the quilt in. I almost forgot."

"Now who's forgetting things?"

"I said *almost*."

"Okay, well," Grandma said. "Tell everyone I say hello."

"You're not coming," I said. "Are *you* avoiding me?"

"Don't be silly, mago. I'm just working hard these days, too—and luckily I have the Kindness Club to fill in for me."

I nodded. "Yeah, okay," I said.

The next morning, I folded up the quilt and slipped it neatly into a brown paper bag. I briefly considered telling Grandma that I didn't feel well enough to go to school. I didn't want to face Chloe and Theo, even though I knew they'd be really kind to me. But still, I didn't feel like facing them. But if I played sick, Grandma probably wouldn't let me go to the Community House after school. She'd think I'd infect the kids or something, and then I'd end up letting them down, too.

On the way to school, Theo told me he'd talked to Vanessa, who'd promised to spread the word to everyone else: Serena's party would be at Chloe's house, still at noon, and still a surprise.

But at lunchtime, we found out that wasn't the case after all.

The first sign of trouble was that Serena didn't come sit at our table. She was with the It Girls instead, and while I was disappointed that she picked lunch with them over the Kindness Club, I understood: Vanessa was there, and Vanessa was her best friend. She was just sitting with her best friend, the way I was sitting with my best friends.

But when I raised my hand to wave to her, she didn't wave back. That was the second sign of trouble.

The third and final sign came when we'd finished eating and were taking our trays over to the conveyor belt. And it wasn't so much a sign as it was an in-your-face, impossible-to-ignore statement. Serena came up to drop her tray, too. She was with Vanessa, plus Rachael, Anjali, and Monroe. Having five of them there was intimidating. Five against three. I was still hoping that there wasn't a problem. But a bad feeling had settled inside me at the bowling alley, and it had been growing bigger and bigger ever since.

It was Monroe who spoke first: "Lucy, Serena has something she wants to tell you."

From the tone of her voice I had a feeling that whatever

Serena wanted to say wasn't going to be good. I tried to ignore that feeling.

"I can tell her if you want," Vanessa offered.

Serena shook her head. "No, I can." She looked at me. "I'm sorry, Lucy."

"You don't have to tell her you're sorry," Monroe interrupted.

"I know you were trying to do a nice thing," Serena went on. "But I don't want my birthday party to be a project for the Kindness Club. That's even worse than the DML."

"Your birthday party? You *know*?"

"I told her," Monroe said.

"But . . . but . . . ," I sputtered.

"I wasn't going to," Monroe said. "But we were talking about her birthday, and she said she didn't want to do anything this year. Then I *had* to tell her, so she'd know not to show up. It's her birthday after all. She should get to decide."

I couldn't argue with that.

"Are you sure?" Chloe asked Serena. "We moved it to my house."

"I know," Serena said. "But I don't want a party anywhere. Okay?"

"Okay," I said. There was nothing else to say.

Vanessa put her arm around Serena. Then Monroe put her arm around the other side. They walked away, and I just stood there, with Chloe and Theo beside me. I couldn't even look at them. I'd told Vanessa and Monroe that they hadn't been treating Serena quite right—that they'd been making her feel worse about her mom. But this whole thing had been my idea, and that meant I'd made her feel the worst of all. My eyes felt hot, and my heart felt like it had been jabbed with the hot dog tongs behind the concession stand at Tanaka Lanes.

The bell rang, and slowly, slowly, I followed Theo and Chloe back to class.

After school, there was only one thing I wanted to do, and that was go home and get under the covers and never come out. I told Chloe and Theo to bring the quilt to the Community House without me.

"Oh, but we couldn't!" Chloe said. "It wouldn't be right. You're the one who did all the work."

"You guys helped."

"Not really. Look at this, Lucy." She pulled a corner out of the bag. I could see the blue tie-dyed back of the quilt, and on the front, the patch that Wendell had made: a lizard breathing fire.

"It didn't come out the way I wanted it to," I told Chloe. "The patches got a little bunched up."

"I didn't even notice," Theo said. "It looks great. It's the best quilt I've ever seen."

"That's only because you haven't seen many," I told him.

"Come on, Lucy," Chloe said. "It wouldn't be the same without you there. And we want to help you feel better—seeing the kids get the quilt would make you feel better. You know that—that's how serotonin works."

I didn't think there was any way my brain could make any serotonin. I was too upset. "Please," I said. "The thing you could do to help me is take the quilt to the kids and just leave me alone. I think I'm an introvert after all."

"No, you're not," Theo said. "You're just an extrovert having a bad day."

"Well, I still need some alone time."

"Okay. Well. I'll call to check on you later, then," Chloe said.

"Me too," Theo said.

"'Bye," I told them.

CHAPTER 22

The next morning, I did something I'd never done. I stayed home from school when I wasn't really sick.

Or maybe I really was sick. I couldn't even tell. I certainly felt horrible. My stomach felt like it was doing a gymnastics show inside my body. My eyes were achy and my head was heavy. Lifting it up off the pillow felt like too much work.

Grandma's hand on my forehead was as cool as a piece of paper. "You don't have a fever," she said. "But I can take you to the doctor if you're unwell."

"No, I don't want to go anywhere," I said, burrowing my face in my bed. "I just want to sleep."

"That's fine," Grandma said. "I'll let Quinnifer's know I have to stay home from work today."

I shook my head in my pillow. "No, you should go," I mumbled.

"What's that, mago?"

I rolled over and pushed myself up on my elbows. "You should go."

"Are you sure? I don't mind. My number-one job is to take care of you."

"I'm not a baby. You don't have to stay home."

"All right, then. You call me if you need anything."

"Okay," I said.

"And I'll let Mrs. Gallagher know that you're home, too."

"Why?"

"Because she's close by," Grandma said. "If you need me, I'll be home as fast as humanly possible. But in an emergency, Mrs. Gallagher can get here even faster."

"I won't need anything," I said, burrowing back down again.

I didn't do anything but lie in bed all morning. Once I'd gotten up to go to the bathroom. And once I'd gone downstairs to get a snack from the kitchen. Grandma had left some rice crackers out on the table, with a Post-it note attached:

These should be
easy on your
stomach.
Love, Grandma

But I didn't feel like eating them. I got a glass of water and headed back upstairs.

When the doorbell rang, the clock on my dresser said it was 12:31. I was still in bed. I hadn't changed into regular clothes, not even plain-looking ones. I grabbed the robe off the hook on my door and went downstairs as the doorbell sounded again.

Grandma didn't say anything about someone coming over to visit. And if it were Dad or Grandma coming to check on me, they'd just use their own keys. I thought back to a "safety assembly" we'd had in the third grade: Don't get into a car with a stranger, don't eat anything a stranger offers you, and don't let a stranger into your house.

I had no plans to let a stranger into my house. I was just going to look through the peephole. If it wasn't someone I knew, I'd call Grandma. No, I'd call the police. And I'd hide in the closet before they got there. Better yet, the bathroom, because there was a lock on the door. I'd lock myself in and wait for help to arrive.

Whoever was at the door started to knock. Three raps.

My heart began to beat faster. Why'd I have to tell Grandma to leave me alone this morning?

I tiptoed toward the door, crouching down so that whoever was outside wouldn't be able to look through the peephole and see me.

But when I looked out, it wasn't a stranger. It was Mrs. Gallagher. I unlocked the door and opened it.

"Hi," I said. "What are you doing here? Are you okay?"

"Oh, yes, dear," Mrs. G said. "I'm absolutely fine. The question is, are *you* okay?"

I shrugged.

She held her arm up to signal she'd brought me something in a brown paper bag. "I took a walk into town and picked up a little soup for you. They say chicken noodle soup has medicinal properties. I'm not sure if that's real or just wishful thinking. Either way, it tastes good."

"Thanks," I said. "Maybe I'll have some a little later."

"Have you eaten anything today?"

"Not really. I've just been sleeping."

"Well, may I come in? I'll fix you a bowl?"

I wanted to say no, but I didn't want to be rude, so I murmured, "mmm hmm" and held the door open wider.

Mrs. G came inside. "The kitchen is this way?" she asked, her body turned toward the right.

"No, it's the other way. Our houses are opposite."

"Well, what do you know? They are."

I followed her into the kitchen. She told me to sit down. It was weird having a guest tell me to take a seat at my own table, but I did as she said. She had a much easier time finding things in my kitchen than I had finding things in hers. She opened a cabinet and closed it. Opened another and found a bowl. I watched her pour in some soup. She brought it over to the table along with a spoon.

"Thank you." I dipped my spoon down and lifted it up to my mouth to take a small slurp.

"Feeling any better?"

"I guess. I'll take a nap again after this. Did you ever have one of those days when you just wanted to fall asleep and wake up when things had changed."

"Yes, dear," Mrs. G said. "But you're too young to feel that way."

"I may be young," I told her. "But I still felt that way. Young people can feel just as bad as old people can—no offense to your age."

"None taken," Mrs. G said. "For what it's worth, sleep wasn't really a solution. I had to learn to keep myself busy in other ways."

"Such as?"

"Such as being friends with you."

"I'm glad we're friends, too," I said. "But I still want to sleep through the rest of fifth grade. Maybe through sixth, too. I tried to do something kind, and it pretty much blew up in my face."

"Oh?"

"Remember the birthday party I wanted to throw for Serena?"

"Of course."

"Well, you were right. We never should've planned one for her. She didn't even want one. But her aunt said yes, as you know, and we told everyone that we were going to have it at the bowling alley. Then, after all that, my dad said we couldn't have it there. Even though he'd already said yes, he said no.

So then Chloe said . . . oh, it doesn't matter what Chloe said. The point is, I let Serena down and now everyone knows about it."

"That sounds like a tough day," Mrs. G said. "But if it was your worst, consider yourself lucky. There are worse things that can happen, and I think you know that."

"I know you mean my mom, but I don't remember that."

"That may be true. But I don't believe for a second that it doesn't affect you."

"I really wanted to do something for Serena, you know? Now I feel so bad. I wasn't even in the mood to take the quilt to the community house yesterday."

"Quilt? What quilt?"

"The kids in the after-school program decorated patches, and I sewed them together."

"I didn't know you quilted. I love quilting."

"It was my first time. It wasn't perfect, but I was excited to give it to the kids. Then all this bad stuff happened, and I didn't want to be kind to anyone. Chloe and Theo brought the quilt over for me. I did zero kind things yesterday, and so far I've done zero today. I'm supposed to do at least three."

"It's hardest to help others when we're feeling our saddest."

"It sure is," I agreed.

"But," Mrs. G went on, "I think that may be when it's most important. We can lift people up as we try to lift up ourselves."

"I didn't even do a very good job on the quilt, if you want to know the truth. It doesn't look like I wanted it to."

"It's the thought that counts, Lucy, and it was a lovely thought," Mrs. G said. "You've had a lot of lovely thoughts lately. You are kind, and your kindness is part of what makes you powerful. But no matter how hard you worked on Serena's birthday—if you had it at the bowling alley, or at Disney World, or even on another planet—you can't change the fact that her mom is gone. It's awful, but there's nothing you can do about it."

"I know. I wasn't trying to. Or I guess I was. But just for that one day. I wish I could go back in time and make it so I never tried in the first place."

"There will always be setbacks, even when you try your hardest. I hope they don't make you stop trying. But this awful feeling you're having right now—that will change, I promise."

"I wish this would change faster."

"Maybe if you did something to help Serena, it would change faster," Mrs. G said.

"But what? I can't change what happened to her mom, just like I can't change what happened to mine."

My mom was in the conversation now. I was the one who brought her in, and I felt the tingles start. The picture of me on Mom's lap flashed into my head. The one where I had one arm around Timber, and one arm lifted up, my fingers in her hair. Mom had her arms around me. She was wearing a cream-colored V-neck sweater. It looked really soft, like maybe it was cashmere or even angora. The kind of thing I'd love to have now, and wrap around myself like a blanket.

"Oh my goodness," I said softly. "Oh my goodness. Oh my goodness."

"What?"

"Did you say you quilted?"

"I did indeed," Mrs. G said. "When my friend Hilda adopted a little boy, I made a quilt for him. That was forty years ago, and I've been quilting ever since."

"This is the best coincidence of all the coincidences," I said.

"What's that?"

"Living next door to an expert quilter," I told her. I didn't want to hide under the covers anymore. "I have an idea."

CHAPTER 23

"You know how I said Serena's aunt took all her mom's clothes to Second Chance?" I said. Mrs. G nodded. "It was because they were making Serena's dad upset to look at. Serena wanted to keep them herself, but they would've taken up too much space in her closet. That's what her aunt Odessa said."

"I think I see where you're going here."

"We can go to Second Chance and buy back Mrs. Kappas's clothes! They can be the patches of a quilt for Serena! Do you think she'd like that?"

"I think she'd love it."

"Yeah, me too," I said. "But she might not. I thought she'd want a party."

"There's a big difference between a surprise party and a surprise present," Mrs. G said. "Maybe she won't want this particular present at this particular time. After Thomas died, there were so many things that reminded me of him that I wasn't ready to look at. Like the bowl of apples in the kitchen."

"But it's in the middle of your table," I said.

"It is *now*," Mrs. G said. "Thomas ate an apple every day of his life, up till the end. When he died, I couldn't look at apples. I avoided the produce aisle at the grocery store, just so I wouldn't have to see them. You have no idea how hard it is to avoid apples—they're everywhere! And they made me feel a bit like you felt this morning."

"What happened to you was worse than Serena not wanting a party," I admitted.

Mrs. G shook her head. "It's not a contest. We all find ourselves hiding in our little holes for different reasons. My point is, I no longer feel that way. In fact, nowadays I *like* looking at apples. I've never been much of an apple eater myself, but you see that I've put out some plastic ones, to remind me."

"I always get tingles when something reminds me of my mom. Or I guess I'm not reminded—I don't remember her. I just remember that she's gone. But I like looking at her picture. I look at it every day."

Mrs. G leaned over and squeezed me to her. She gave me a little kiss on the top of my head. "Shall we get those clothes, then?"

"I just thought of a problem. A big one. I was so excited

about my idea, and I totally forgot that things at Second Chance cost money. I don't have much. I definitely don't have enough to buy back all of Mrs. Kappas's clothes."

"Lucky for you, I happen to have some money of my own," Mrs G. said.

I shook my head. "I only get ten dollars a week for allowance. Well, actually, nine dollars. And my dad isn't always great at remembering to give it to me. It would take me too long to pay you back."

"Nonsense. You don't have to pay me back."

"Of course I would!" I said. "You don't even know Serena. I can't let you spend your money on her mother's clothes."

"I'd be doing it for you, dear, not for Serena. Well, a little bit for Serena, too, because I know what it's like to lose someone important. But mostly for you. You and your friends have been tending to my yard free of charge these past few weeks. I owe a lot to you."

"We didn't do it to get paid, and you don't owe us anything. We did it to be kind."

"And now I'm doing this to be kind," Mrs. G said. "Come on, let's call your grandmother and see if she'll give you permission to leave the house on this supposed sick day. I suspect it's not much of a sick day anymore."

"No, it's not," I said. I smiled. "Thank you, Mrs. G. You're right about chicken soup. I feel so much better."

Grandma said it was okay for me to take a walk with Mrs. G, as long as I was feeling up to it. Which I was, of course. I was feeling better, though also sad. The whole time I was planning Serena's bowling party, I was so excited about surprising her that I'd forgotten a bit about what made it so sad. And now the sadness was there. Serena's mom was dead. We were going to Second Chance to buy back her clothes. Clothes she herself would never get to wear again. But at least Serena could have them, and they could cover her like a blanket when she really needed her mom. Having things from your parents isn't the same as having them right there with you. But this was the most I could do.

The bell above the door to Second Chance rang as we walked in. A woman named Nicki was working behind the desk. She was a designer like me—she made her own jewelry, and she knew how sometimes you need to look around for a long time when you're waiting for inspiration to strike.

But there was no time for that today. After we said our hellos, I filled her in on our mission. "Can you tell us which clothes were Mrs. Kappas's, so we can buy them all back?"

"I wish I could, sweetheart," Nicki said. "But I don't keep track of who donates what."

"Oh no," I said. "Are you sure? It would've been a woman named Odessa. I don't know what she looks like, but her niece has long dark hair and green eyes, so maybe she does, too.

She would've come in . . . well, I don't know when she came in, but it had to be at least a week and a day ago, because that's when I heard Serena talking about it."

"I'm sorry," Nicki said. "It's the change of seasons right now, which means a lot of people have been bringing things. But the good news is, I haven't had time to separate things out of the bags yet. If you want to look through them, maybe you'll find the bag of clothes that belonged to your friend's mom."

"I didn't know Serena's mom," I said sadly. "So I don't know what her clothes looked like." I shook my head. "Thanks anyway."

Mrs. G put a hand on my shoulder. "Now, now," she said. "Let's just take a look. You never know what will spark a memory."

I knew I wasn't going to suddenly remember Mrs. Kappas's clothes, but I followed Mrs. G to the back of the store anyway. Usually I love going through the discards at Second Chance. You never know what you're going to find. But now I halfheartedly lifted a flap on the first bag of clothes and glanced in: some jeans, a few T-shirts, an old leather jacket, a white blouse with a stain on the collar. Could these have belonged to Mrs. Kappas? Maybe. Maybe not. I didn't think so.

"Nothing is familiar," I said.

"Check the next bag," Mrs. G said.

I did. It was full of baby clothes. So not that one. And the next bag, a mix of stuff for men and women. I didn't think it was that one, either, since Aunt Odessa had only given Serena's mom's stuff away. The bag after that was mostly women's stuff, but I didn't recognize anything. Not that I expected to.

"Mrs. G, I feel bad," I said. "This was such a good idea, but it's not going to work out. I'm just wasting your time."

But she just nudged me toward the next bag. "Come on," she said. "Only three more to go."

The next bag had a lot of corduroy pants and turtlenecks. I wondered who had bought them. Was it Serena's mom? Was she someone who wore corduroys and turtlenecks? Or was it someone else who just went through a corduroy-pants-and-turtleneck phase, and then decided that wasn't her thing anymore, so they ended up here. I didn't know. I shrugged at Mrs. G.

"Second-to-last one," she said. I lifted the flap and looked in. There were flannel pajamas, an old concert T-shirt, some pairs of pants, a couple sweaters, a scarf with elephants on it.

A scarf with elephants on it.

A SCARF WITH ELEPHANTS ON IT!

"Mrs. G! This is the bag!"

"You sure?"

"Serena talked about this scarf in her grief group! I heard her! And she mentioned something else . . . a silk blouse.

A pink one." I bent back down and rummaged through the rest of the bag. "It's not in here, though."

"Perhaps her aunt hung on to it."

"No, Serena specifically said she gave it away."

"Well, there's one bag left."

"Right! It'll be in there—I just know it. After all, Serena's aunt must've brought in more than one bag of clothes—she was bringing in a whole wardrobe!"

I dug into the remaining bag of clothes, and lo and behold, there it was: Mrs. Kappas's pink silk blouse. I clutched it in my hands, the material soft between my fingers. I wondered when Serena's mom had worn it last, and whether it had been washed afterward. If we looked at it under a special micro-scope, would we be able to see her fingerprints? How long do fingerprints last, after a person herself is gone?

"You okay?" Mrs. G asked.

"I was just thinking," I said. "You know how when a day is done, it's done forever?"

"Yes."

"I think that's why I like shopping here."

"I'm afraid I don't follow."

"People who wore these clothes were done with them. Maybe they died, or maybe they grew out of them, or maybe they just didn't like them anymore. But here we are buy-ing them, so they're not really done. It's like giving an old day a second chance—like the store says. Does that make sense?"

"It's just about the best explanation I've ever heard," Mrs. G told me. "Come on, let's pay."

"It's really a lot. I hope it's not too expensive."

"I'll worry about the cost," Mrs. G said. "You worry about bringing these bags to the front of the store."

CHAPTER 24

Nicki did the most amazing thing. She gave us the clothes for free. Mrs. G had her wallet out and was all ready to pay, but Nicki told her to put it away. I thought back to something our principal, Mr. Dibble, had told Chloe, Theo, and me, when we told him about the Kindness Club. He said kindness was a bit like the butterfly effect. You do an act of kindness, and you never get to know the extent of its effect. Its ripples go on and on. But right there, I could trace some things back to our original kindness: we'd helped Mrs. G with her yard, and now she'd tried to do something for Serena. And all that happened to Nicki was she heard about it, and she wanted to do something, too.

"I hope the quilt brings your friend some comfort," Nicki told me.

"Thank you," I said.

One thing Mrs. G *did* pay for was the cab ride home. I don't think it had anything to do with the driver being kind or unkind, but he didn't know the whole story. We got dropped off on the street right in front of our houses, and I lugged Mrs. Kappas's clothes up the walkway to my front door. Mrs. G offered to help, but I was afraid she'd hurt her back. So I did it by myself, first one bag, then the other.

"Why don't you call your grandmother and let her know we're home," Mrs. G told me. "I want to grab a few things I have at my place. I'll be back in a few minutes."

I left the bags in the front hall, right by the bottom of the stairs, and went into the kitchen to get the phone. I was just about to pick it up to dial Grandma at the bowling alley when it started ringing. Another coincidence. I didn't even check the caller ID before I picked up the phone. "Hey, Grandma," I said. "That's so crazy—I was just about to call you!"

"Lucy?" a man's voice said.

It wasn't Dad's voice, and it wasn't Oliver's. "Who is this?"

"It's Felix. Felix Martinez. I used to work with your father at the bowling alley. You remember me, right?"

"Yeah," I said. "I remember. My dad's not home right now."

"I figured that," Felix said. "I didn't want to bother him at work. I thought if I called the house I'd get voice mail."

He probably didn't want to speak to Dad live because he was embarrassed about leaving him in the lurch. Maybe the message he planned to leave was to say sorry.

"No school today?" Felix asked me.

"There's still school," I said. "I just wasn't feeling well."

"I'm sorry to hear that. I hope you feel better soon."

"Thank you." I was trying to be polite, but it was hard. I was mad at Dad, but I was even madder at Felix. If he hadn't quit without notice, Dad wouldn't have been so stressed these last couple weeks, and our big blowup at the bowling alley never would've happened.

But then, I wouldn't have stayed home from school, and Mrs. G certainly wouldn't have offered to buy back Mrs. Kappas's clothes.

So maybe I wasn't that mad after all. Sometimes it's hard to decide how to feel.

"Are you well enough to jot down a message for your dad?" Felix asked.

"Yeah."

"Tell me when you're ready."

Grandma kept a pad in the drawer beside the utensils. I pulled it out, along with one of the pens that said Tanaka Lanes on the side. "I'm ready," I told Felix.

"You tell your dad that I appreciate the call he made to the fitness center. I just found out that the job is mine."

I'd started writing, but I paused, and the pen made a dark point on the page. "Wait a second," I said. "You *just* got a new job? Like today?"

"Thanks to your dad, I did," Felix said. "Can you tell him that?"

"Uh-huh."

"And tell him my fingers are crossed that things start looking up at Tanaka Lanes."

"Do you mean . . . do you mean things were looking down?"

"Uh," Felix said. "Hey, Lucy, let's just rewind the tape and pretend I didn't say that."

"You can't rewind and go back," I told Felix. "You can't change the past. You can only change the future."

"You're a smart kid," he said. "Too smart for my own good. I think I should let you go."

"No, wait," I said. "Felix?"

"Yeah?"

"You didn't quit working at the bowling alley, did you?"

Felix gave a nervous laugh. "I'll tell you something," he said. "Tanaka Lanes is a special place. You should be proud of your dad."

I felt something in the back of my throat. Like I'd taken a bite of a Tanaka dog, swallowed funny, and now it was stuck there. "I am proud," I said.

"If he's ever hiring again, I want him to give me a call. You tell him that."

The doorbell rang. Mrs. G was back.

"You got that, Lucy?" Felix asked.

"Yeah. I got it."

"Feel better, kiddo."

"Thanks," I said.

CHAPTER 25

I barely had time to think about what Felix had said, because Mrs. G and I had so much work to do. She said the quilt would have three layers: First, a top layer of patches stitched together. Second, a middle layer called batting, which was basically a filler to give the quilt some weight. And third, a back layer to hold it all together.

Luckily, Mrs. G had brought batting and fabric for the back. As for the top layer, we had Mrs. Kappas's clothes. I dumped the bags out in the living room. There was so much stuff, the entire living room floor was covered, as if a closet had exploded. All the things Serena's mom used to wear. There was the scarf, and the pink blouse. Plus so much more. "I don't see any socks or underwear," I told Mrs. G. "She must've had some. It seems weird that those would be the only things that Odessa decided to keep."

"My guess is she threw them away," Mrs. G said.

"Secondhand places don't usually sell that sort of thing. I guess even those of us looking for a bargain don't want to own used socks and underwear."

"The pioneers would have taken them," I told her.

"The pioneers?" Mrs. G asked. "You mean the people who settled in the west a couple hundred years ago?"

"We're studying them in school," I said. "They used whatever they could to keep warm and survive, and sometimes it wasn't enough."

"We're lucky to be alive now," Mrs. G said.

"Yeah," I agreed. "But look—" I swept my arm out, gesturing to all the clothes on the floor. "Serena's mom had plenty to wear and keep her warm, and she still died."

"That's surely true," Mrs. G said. "It's hard to make sense of things sometimes, isn't it?"

"It really is."

We got started. Mrs. G had a special acrylic ruler, which she opened up on the coffee table, to measure out five-and-a-half-inch squares. We each had a pair of fabric scissors to cut the squares. It took a long time because they had to be perfect. When we finished, Mrs. G wanted to lay them out on the floor in the right order, so we could see what the quilt would look like. But with her bad back, it was hard for her to bend over, so she directed me: "Let's alternate a light square, then a dark square, light, then dark . . . Hmm, no, I'm not sure I like that one there. Move the yellow up to the top—no, not that one. *That* one. There you go . . . Okay, I like that, but the middle has way too much pink right now. Let's move a few of those squares around."

I didn't realize how much work went into figuring out the placement of the quilt patches. We'd been at it for a half hour when the doorbell rang again.

"You expecting someone?" Mrs. G asked.

"I don't think so." I stood up and headed to the front hall, feeling much less nervous this time around, since I had Mrs. G right there with me. When I looked through the peephole, Chloe and Theo were standing on the porch steps. I unlocked the door and threw it open.

"I'm so glad you're here!" I told them.

"We wanted to check on you," Chloe said. "Plus we brought the weekend homework for you. Not that you should worry too much about homework if you're sick. But we thought maybe you were just upset about the last couple of days, and that's why you stayed home. Don't worry—we didn't tell Ms. Danos we thought that. We didn't talk to anyone about it besides each other."

"I'm feeling much better now," I said.

"Are you sure?" Theo asked. "You look a little flushed. He took a step back. "Do you think you're contagious?"

"Definitely not," I said. "I'm completely cured, and I need your help—both of you."

I pulled Chloe and Theo into the living room. They said

hi to Mrs. G, and looked shocked by the project on the living room floor. We told them all about it. Of course they thought it was a great idea and wanted to help. But first Chloe had to use the kitchen phone to call her mom and let her know where she was. Then Theo called his parents. Then I called Grandma to belatedly let her know we were home, since I hadn't done that before.

I'd completely forgotten about the call with Felix up until that moment. I could hear Mrs. G in the other room, explaining the next steps: "We finally settled on the placement of the squares. So if you two agree, we'll move on to the next step, which is pinning them together row by row." I wanted to talk to Grandma about what Felix had said, but now wasn't the time.

"You okay, mago?" Grandma asked.

"I am," I said. "Chloe and Theo came over to bring my homework, and they're staying to help us with the quilt."

"Just don't overdo it."

"I won't. I promise."

I headed back to the living room to help pin things together. It was already starting to look like a quilt.

Mrs. G asked me to bring down the iron and the ironing board. Luckily, I didn't have to use them myself. My job was the sewing machine. I ran the first row through, attaching square to square to square.

"Wow," Chloe said. "I never realized how much work sewing is. It's amazing how you make all your own clothes."

"Not *all* of them," I said.

"But a lot of them."

"Yeah. It's hard work, but it's worth it," I said, and I ran the next square under the needle.

After about a half hour, the first row was finally done, and I handed it over to Chloe. Mrs. G told her how to iron them to get the seams all facing the same way. Meanwhile, I'd moved on to stitching the second row. It went a little bit faster than the first, but not much.

"We have so many rows to do," I said when I finally finished. "We're never going to get this done by Sunday."

"You have to eat the elephant one bite at a time," Mrs. G said.

"Elephant?!" I cried. "I'd never eat an elephant!"

"It's a metaphor," Theo told me. "It means when you have a big project, you need to go one step at a time."

"Precisely," Mrs. G said. "Don't worry about the finished product just now. We'll do it square by square. Do you want me to take over for the third row?"

"Yes, please," I said.

While she did that, I measured out and cut the fabric that would make the border and the binding, while Chloe and Theo started cleaning up the leftover scraps of clothing, stuffing them back into the garbage bags. On my first quilt, I didn't even use a border or a binding, but I quickly realized why Mrs. G thought we needed them. They were the final pieces that would hold everything together and make the quilt look professional. But we weren't even close to the final steps yet. We'd only made it through half the rows when the front door opened. "Hello, anyone home?"

"Dad!" I called. "We're in here!"

Mrs. G stood up from the sewing machine and shook Dad's hand hello. "What's all this?" he asked.

"We're making a quilt to bring to Serena," I said. "I know it looks a little messy, but I'll clean it all. Don't worry."

"I wasn't worried," Dad said.

"Oh," I said. "That's cool."

"Cool Dad strikes again." I wasn't sure if he was kidding or not, but then he smiled, so I gave a little smile, too.

"Where's Grandma?" I asked. "At the alley?"

"No, we closed for the night."

"Closed?" It was barely dinnertime on a Friday night. Usually the alley stayed open late on Fridays and Saturdays. People liked to bowl when they didn't have school or work to wake up for. "Why?"

"Grandma's taking a night off," Dad said, not answering. "She's been working so hard lately. I thought she should go out with a couple of friends, and that gave me an excuse to have dinner with you."

"Oh, no," Chloe said. "Are we intruding? I can call my mom to pick me up. She doesn't like me to walk home this late."

"No intrusion at all," Dad said. "We're adding to the menu at Tanaka Lanes. I brought food home to try. There's plenty for everyone."

I set the table in the kitchen for the five of us. Dad had Tanaka dogs and Tanaka burgers, plus chicken wings with a bunch of different dipping sauces, cheese sticks, wrap sandwiches, and even sushi.

"This is quite an assortment, Ken," Mrs. G said.

"We're thinking of building out the restaurant to attract a bigger crowd," Dad explained. "A potential chef came today with some samples. He thought sushi might be a nice touch, given the name of the alley. Though that's something we're thinking of changing, too."

"Tanaka Lanes might not be Tanaka Lanes anymore?" I asked. "Then what would it be?"

"That's all up for debate," Dad said. "Lots of changes are coming, so I'll need your votes on the food."

I tried a little bit of everything, except the salmon sushi— Chloe and I both opted out of eating that. I did it for Poseidon, of course. Chloe didn't know Ollie's fish, but she didn't want to eat it, either. "I'm sure it's really good, as salmon goes," she assured Dad, "but I tasted it recently, and it wasn't really my thing."

"No worries," Dad told her. "Different folks, different strokes."

"Actually," Theo said, "the secret to liking new food is repetition. You have to taste it like nine or ten times." He popped a piece of sushi in his mouth.

"What do you think?" Dad asked.

Theo chewed and chewed and chewed, and finally

swallowed. "I think I need to taste it a few more times," he admitted, and he picked up a cheese stick.

The phone rang, and Dad stood to answer it. It was Chloe's mom, calling from the car. She was on her way. We were pretty much finished with dinner, but I was still disappointed that Chloe was leaving. There was so much left to do on the quilt.

"One person down," I said. I turned to Dad. "Unless you can help Theo, Mrs. G, and me."

"I'm afraid it's time for me to head home as well," Mrs. G said. "It's been a long day."

"But Mrs. G—"

"Hey, Goose," Dad cut in. "I believe the words you're looking for are 'thank you.'"

"Yeah, of course. If you're tired you should go home. And thank you for everything. Really."

"You're welcome," Mrs. G said.

"Just out of curiosity, how long does it usually take you to make a quilt?"

"It depends on the quilt," Mrs. G said. "Some quilts take a month."

"A month? We don't have that kind of time."

"I've done some in a week's time."

"Serena's birthday is *Sunday*." I was trying to keep the disappointment out of my voice, because I knew Mrs. G had done a lot for me. But still. I supposed we could get the quilt to Serena *after* her birthday. It just wouldn't be the same.

"It's going to be tight, I know," Mrs. G said. "But this quilt has four workers on it, not just one. I'll take a couple rows home with me. Sometimes I wake up in the middle of the night, and I may as well fire up my own sewing machine. I'll come over here in the morning."

"I'll come over, too," Chloe said.

"So will I," Theo added.

"How does that sound, Lucy?" Mrs. G asked.

"It sounds great," I said, and I meant it.

A horn honked outside. Chloe's mom had arrived. She was going to take Theo home, too. He only lived a block away, but it was too late for him to walk on his own. We said good-bye, and they left with Mrs. G.

Then it was just Dad and me. It had been a long time since I was alone with my dad, and even though he was my dad, I felt a little nervous about it. It was a strange feeling. After all, he'd been my dad for a decade. What did I have to feel nervous about?

"What do you say we tackle these dishes before Grandma gets home?" Dad asked. "If she comes in before we're done, she'll take over, and I want her night off to actually be a night off."

"Sure," I said. "I have a lot of experience doing dishes lately."

Dad sighed and shook his head. "A new dishwasher is going to cost several hundred dollars," he said. "We'll get one when we get one. Money doesn't grow on trees, Lucy."

"I know that," I said. "I wasn't complaining about it. I just meant—I'm getting good at doing the dishes. That's all."

To prove it, I stepped up to the sink, turned on the hot water, and donned Grandma's rubber gloves.

"You wash, I'll dry?" Dad asked.

"Sure," I said.

We worked quietly side by side for a couple minutes, and then Dad cleared his throat. "I'm sorry if I snapped at you," he said. "I think I've been short with you a few times these last couple weeks. I didn't mean to be. And to answer your question, I think Grandma and I are going to go next weekend to pick up a new dishwasher, so you'll only be on dish duty for another week. Sound okay?"

"Yeah, but you don't have to. I don't mind dish duty if it's too expensive. Plus it gives me something kind to do. I need at least three a day."

"Is that a club rule?"

"Yeah," I said. "But I think I'm the only one counting."

"Well, I'm happy for the help," Dad said. "And things will get easier from this point forward, I think."

"That's good." I paused, scrubbing some blue cheese sauce off a plate with the scrub brush. "Dad? Felix called today."

"He did, did he?"

"Uh-huh. He said to tell you he got the job at the fitness center, thanks to you."

"I'm really glad to hear that."

"Felix didn't quit without giving you notice, did he?" I asked. "He didn't quit at all."

Dad dried off the plate that was in his hands and put it on the counter. We weren't done washing and drying yet, but he folded the towel he'd been using, and placed it next to the plate. "Come sit down," he said.

I turned off the faucet and took off my gloves. Dad pulled out my chair, and after I sat down, he sat down, too. "No, Lucy," he said. "Felix didn't quit. I had to let him go. Believe me, I didn't want to. It was the most painful business decision I've ever had to make. But business hasn't been good, and I've been cutting corners to try and save the alley."

My stomach tightened. Of course. I'd known that's what it was. Ever since Felix had called, I'd known it. Even before that, I'd sort of known. I just hadn't wanted to.

But it was one thing to think something in your head, and another to hear it out loud. As long as it was in my head, it didn't have to be true. Now Dad had said it. I was afraid for him to answer the question I wanted to ask next. But I took a deep breath and asked it anyway: "Is it saved?"

"Yes," Dad said. "As a matter of fact, I think it is."

"Oh, thank goodness," I said. I let out a breath. *Phew.* "How come you don't sound happy about it?"

"I am happy about it," Dad said. "But I'm sad, too, because I had to make certain sacrifices. I'm not the sole owner of Tanaka Lanes anymore."

"I don't understand," I said. "It's called Tanaka Lanes."

But as I said the words, I remembered something he'd said over dinner. "Wait, is that why there might be a name change?"

"It's part of the reason," Dad said. "An investment group bought a percentage of the business, which means they own part of it and I own part of it."

"How much do they own?"

"Assuming the deal goes through on Monday, they'll own ninety percent."

"Ninety percent!" I cried. "That's practically the whole thing."

"Be grateful it's not the whole thing. That's what they wanted. I didn't want to give up a business that I worked so hard to build. Thanks to your grandmother, I've been bowling my entire life. Having Tanaka Lanes was a dream come true. But the alley needs money right now—and I don't have money to give."

"I wish I could speed up time and be all grown up already," I told Dad. "Then I'd be a famous designer, and I'd have plenty of money to give you."

"Let's not speed up time, okay?" Dad said. "You'll be grown up soon enough. And when you are, it won't be your job to fix this."

"Sure it will be," I told him. "It's important to help your family out. Like Grandma helped you take care of Ollie and me, and at the bowling alley."

"You take after your grandmother," he said. "Your instinct is always to help out where you can. I'm so proud of you. But part of being an effective helper is knowing your own limits."

"You mean some things I can change, and some things I can't," I said, and he nodded. "But eventually everything changes all on its own, you know."

"I know," Dad said.

"I'm sorry I called you unkind," I told him. "I know you're not. You've always been a kind person, and I know you would've let us have a party if you could've."

"Once things are running smoothly back at the alley again, you can invite your friends," Dad said. "Maybe we can throw together a belated birthday party for Serena. I know it's not the same as a party on the actual day, but we can make it special."

"Thanks, but we don't have to. Serena doesn't want a party after all."

"Oh?"

"I thought if I made her birthday really special, she'd have a day when she didn't have to miss her mom so much. Like on my birthdays, I don't miss Mom. I have you, and Grandma, and when Ollie was home, I had him, too."

"You still have Oliver," Dad said. "He went to college, but he didn't disappear completely."

"It's still different now," I said.

"Yes, it is," Dad said.

"And I do miss Mom. I think I miss her more than I used to. It's been longer since she's been gone, and the missing part is getting worse. Sometimes I just say that I don't because then it's easier."

"How is it easier?" Dad asked.

"It's like if you're a kid and a stranger sees you, that stranger will say, 'Where's your mom?' because most kids have moms. I never say the truth—I never say that my mom is dead. I just say, 'She's not here,' or 'I'm actually looking for my dad,' or Grandma, or whoever. Because I don't want to make them feel bad. But if you want to know the truth, it makes *me* feel bad. Not having a mom stinks. It really stinks."

"I know it does," Dad said.

"I don't even remember her, and that makes it worse. Like she was never mine."

"She was yours, Lucy. And you were hers. I promise. I was there."

"Can I tell you something else?" Dad nodded. "It makes me a teeny bit jealous of Serena. I know that's crazy, because Serena doesn't have her mom anymore, either, but at least she has memories of her. I only have memories that come from pictures. Like, I can almost feel the way her hair was, but it's just because I've looked at the picture of my first birthday so much. But it's not a real memory. If it was, I'd remember other things from that day, too."

"I can tell you anything you want to know."

"I want to know everything," I said. "And even more

than that, I want to know what it was like on the days that there aren't any pictures. Do you remember those?"

"Of course I do," Dad said.

"Tell me something."

Dad reached out and put a hand on my hand. "She was the first person to call you Goose," he said. "It started out as 'Lucy-Goosey,' when you were a brand-new baby, but pretty soon it shortened to Goose. I wouldn't have been surprised if you thought that was your actual name."

"I think I did," I said. "Maybe."

"And she taught you to say 'quack,'" he went on. "It was, maybe, your third word. I told her that geese technically honk at one another, and she said she knew, but she thought quacking was cuter. And as far as your mother was concerned, nothing in the world was as cute as you—except Oliver. I have to agree with her on that."

"Do you think she'd be proud of me now?" I asked.

"Of course," Dad said. "She'd be very proud of you."

"Would she be okay with my clothes, or would she have tried to get me to dress like everyone else?"

"Your mom didn't want any kid but you," Dad said. "You were the child of her dreams, and she's a part of your life now, even though she's not here in person. Every time I look at you, I see parts of her. Your eyes, and the slope of your nose, and the little furrow you get in your forehead, like you're getting right now. And when you laugh, you sound exactly like her. Maybe it's easier for me, because I get to remember your mom every day, every single time I look at you."

I nodded. I didn't speak because I had started to cry.

Dad reached up to wipe a tear away. "And another thing, Lucy," he said.

"What?" I whisper-asked.

"You're the child of my dreams, too."

CHAPTER 26

My fingers had never been so sore. The tips were red, and there were dots of blood where I'd accidentally stabbed myself with a needle.

It was Sunday evening. It would still be Serena's birthday for a few more hours, and the quilt was done.

It had taken round-the-clock sewing by Chloe, Theo, Mrs. G, and me. Dad and Grandma helped, too, in between shifts at work. So did Chloe's mom, and Theo's parents and his sister, and even Vanessa Medina. We called her Saturday afternoon, because we knew we needed more help. Back when we were planning the party, Vanessa had said she wanted to help us out. We took a chance that that was still the case, and she said yes.

Mrs. G gave her a row to work on. "Wow, I remember this shirt," Vanessa said, fingering a black-and-white-checked square. "Daphne wore it to our spring dance showcase."

"Do you think Serena won't want the quilt?" I asked. "Like, will it be too hard for her?"

"Nah," Vanessa said. "I think she'll love it more than any other present. All I got her was a geode."

"Geodes are cool," Chloe said.

"I don't know what they are," I admitted.

"They look like ordinary rocks on the outside," Theo said. "But break them open and there are crystals that formed from cavities in the rocks millions of years ago."

"Serena collects them," Vanessa said. "I still think the quilt is better."

"Well, you're helping," I told her. "That means it's from you, too."

For dinner that night, Vanessa's parents sent over a bunch of foot-long subs for us to share. There were so many people doing so many kindnesses. It was amazing. Sometimes when you're just going through your life, you don't notice how much kindness there is. But if you look around, the opportunities for kindness and the people being kind are everywhere.

Our team kept pinning, and ironing, and sewing, and we got it done. I thought we should let everyone who helped come with us to deliver the quilt, but Mrs. Barnes said she thought that would be too overwhelming. Almost like having a party, which we knew she didn't want. Instead, she called the Kappases' house to say happy birthday to Serena, and she told her we had a present for her. "Theo and the girls can drop it off this evening, if that's all right," Mrs. Barnes said.

Serena said a drop-off would be okay, so Mrs. Barnes drove us over. Just the three of us—Theo, Chloe, and me. The last thing we'd done when we'd finished the quilt was sew on a tag. It didn't say "Designed by Lucy." It said, "Designed by Your Friends." Then we folded the quilt and tied it with a big red bow. On the way over to the Kappases', I held it in a big brown shopping bag on my lap, but when I stepped out of the car onto the driveway, I realized I didn't want to be the one to hand it to Serena. I was proud of it, and I was excited for Serena to have it, but I wanted someone else to carry it.

Shy is not something I feel very often. But I felt it right then. "Here," I said, holding the bag out toward Chloe. "You give it to her."

"You don't want to?"

I shook my head.

"I don't want to, either," Chloe said. "I've never given a present to someone whose mom just died."

We looked over at Theo. "Don't look at me," he said.

"Kids," Mrs. Barnes said. "Serena is exactly the same kid she was last week and last month and last year."

"Actually, ninety-eight percent of the atoms in your body are replaced every year," Theo said. "So she's not exactly the same."

Mrs. Barnes shook her head. "Would you like me to carry it?"

"Yes, please," I said.

But before I handed it over, the front door opened. We hadn't even had a chance to ring the doorbell, and there Serena was. She was in jeans and a long-sleeved blue top. An ordinary outfit, like it was an ordinary day, not a birthday at all.

Mrs. Barnes walked up the front steps, without taking the package from me. Not that it mattered, since Serena could see me holding it. I watched Mrs. Barnes hug her hello. Theo and Chloe went up to say hello, so I did, too. We all muttered "happy birthday." Then we stood awkwardly in the doorway, not knowing what to say, as if we were meeting Serena for the very first time.

A man walked up behind Serena. I knew it was her dad even before he said, "Hey, there. I'm Alec. Who do we have here?"

"These are my friends from school," Serena said. "You know Theo, and this is Lucy, and Chloe."

He mussed Theo's hair, and Chloe and I shook his hand. "Nice handshake," he told me.

"Thanks."

"Would you all like to come in? Serena's aunt and brothers are picking up food right now. I can promise you it'll be more than we can eat ourselves."

"That's all right," Mrs. Barnes said. "We're not staying long. The kids have something for Serena."

I handed the bag over. "This is from all of us."

Serena pulled out the quilt and untied the ribbon. "Oh," she said, her voice sounding almost like an inhale of breath. "It's my . . ."

"That looks like Daphne's sweater," Serena's dad said.

"It is," Serena said. She unfolded the quilt right there on the stoop. "And her skirt, and her shawl, and everything else." She looked back at me. "Where did you get this?"

"I got the clothes from Second Chance," I said. "Then we sewed them together."

"Lucy did most of it," Chloe said.

"No, it was a group effort. Our families helped, and my neighbor, Mrs. G, and even Vanessa. We wanted you to have the best quilt, and we wanted you to have it today."

Serena had started to cry a little bit. I hoped I hadn't made another mistake. I didn't think so, but I couldn't be certain. After all, I'd thought a party was a good idea, too.

"Is it okay that we made it? I don't want to upset you. Mrs. G said if you're not ready to have it right now, you could put it in your closet for later. Or I guess if you don't even want it in your closet, I could put it in mine. I have a really small closet, but there's room in my brother's since he's away at college."

Serena shook her head. "It's okay that you made it. More than okay."

"Good, I'm glad."

"I remember this jean jacket," Mrs. Barnes said, fingering a square. "Daphne wore it all the time. I bet she wore it to at least half the lunch dates we ever had."

"I could've just asked you to help me figure out what clothes were hers in Second Chance," I said. "We went through every bag—they were in the last bag we looked in. Well, the last two bags"

"Well, of course they were in the last bags," Theo said. "Why would you keep looking through bags after you found them?"

Everyone laughed a little bit, even Serena. "You all went through so much trouble for me," she said.

"I think I can speak for the kids when I say it was no trouble at all," Mrs. Barnes told her. She pulled a tissue out of her purse and handed it over.

Serena wiped her face. "I still can't believe you guys did this. Especially after I was rude about not wanting a party. I'm really sorry about that."

"The definition of rude is being offensively impolite or ill-mannered," Theo said. "You weren't either of those things. You simply informed us of your preference. That's nothing to be sorry about."

"Definitely not," Chloe agreed.

"Yeah," I said. "I'm sorry that we tried to have one when you didn't want one. We wanted to do something kind for you, and give you a party so you'd have a good memory of today. Sometimes I play memories in my head like they're movies. I have all these birthday memory movies and my mom isn't in them, but I still like thinking about them. Theo says it's called Kuffino."

"Kopfkino," Theo corrected. "It means head cinema."

"Oh, I definitely have a head cinema," Serena said. "I've been thinking about all my other birthdays today."

"Maybe one day you'll think about this one," Alec Kappas said. "You'll remember what your friends did for you."

"Yeah, I will," Serena said. "I love this quilt so much. Getting it is exactly the birthday memory I want. I mean, if I can't have the one I really want."

I knew what she meant: she wanted another birthday memory that included her mother really being there.

"Can I tell you something?" I asked.

"Yeah, sure."

"My dad and I were talking about my mom the other night, and he said that she's a part of my life, even though she's not here in person. It's the same for your mom. I mean, your mom is not a part of *my* life. But she's a part of yours."

Serena's eyes were shiny, and she wiped at them again with Mrs. Barnes's tissue. "Maybe one day you can tell me things about your mom, and I can tell you things about mine," she said.

"Yeah, I'd like that," I said. "I don't know much, but I'm learning."

After that, Odessa and Serena's brothers came home, and it was time for us to go. We hugged Serena and her dad good-bye, and got back into the car.

"That was a wonderful thing you kids did," Mrs. Barnes said. "It was truly kind."

"That's why we named our club the Kindness Club," Theo said.

"I hope you three are members forever," Mrs. Barnes said.

"Me too," I said, "But the truth is, you can't be anything forever. Things always change."

"No, they don't," Chloe said.

"Yeah, they do," Theo said. "Even scientific theories change. That's why discoveries are best called 'theories' and not 'laws.' Laws are static, and theories are not."

"Well, this won't change," Chloe insisted. "We'll always have each other. Even when we grow up and go away to college and get jobs. We'll still always be in this club. It's a lifetime membership and our brand is . . . c'mon, Lucy. Our brand is—"

"Kindness," I supplied.

"One more time—louder for the folks in the back." I smiled, because of course *we* were the folks in the back. "Our brand is—"

"Kindness!" Theo and I shouted.

"I like it," Mrs. Barnes said.

"Hey, you know what I was thinking?" Chloe said, her voice softened from cheer mode. "I'd like to hear stories about your mom, too."

"So would I," Theo said. "I wish I'd met her. But hearing about her would be the next best thing. If you don't mind."

I didn't mind. I told them.

To my entire crew of kind and generous friends: Lindsay Aaronson, Andrew Baum, Libba Bray, Michael Buckley, Jen Calonita, Erin Cummings, Gitty Daneshvari, Tommy DeGrezia, Julia DeVillers, Melissa Brown Eisenberg, Rachel Feld, the Fleischman/Tofsky family, Gayle Forman, Jackie Friedland, Jake Glaser, Peter Glassman, Mary Gordon, Corey Ann Haydu, Emily Heddleson, Lexa Hillyer, the Leib family (hi, Lily!), Logan Levkoff, Melissa Losquadro, Wendy Mass, Samantha Moss, Stacia Robitaille, Jennie Rosenberg, Jess Rothenberg, Leila Sales, Jill Santopolo, Laura Schechter, Yael Schick, Rebecca Serle, Danielle Sheeler, Jennifer E. Smith, Katie Stein, J. Courtney Sullivan, Rebecca and Jeremy Wallace-Segall, Robin Wasserman, and Christine Whelan.

To my father, Joel Sheinmel; to my mother, Elaine Sheinmel, and my stepdad, Phil Getter; to my sister, Alyssa Sheinmel, and my brother-in-law, JP Gravitt; and to my stepsiblings, their spouses, and most especially the five best nieces and nephews in the world: Nicki, Andrew, and Zach Liss, and Sara and Tesa Getter. I love you guys so much you can't even measure it.

Finally, I want to acknowledge Elizabeth Glaser, whom I miss, and her Pediatric AIDS Foundation cofounders, Susan DeLaurentis and Susie Zeegen, who are my role models for what it means to be a devoted friend.

My heart is full of love and gratitude.

XOXOXO,
Courtney

★ ACKNOWLEDGMENTS ★

Thank you to the extraordinary members of my very own kindness club—

To Laura Dail, who is an incredible agent and an even better friend; and to her colleagues at the Laura Dail Literary Agency, Inc., especially Tamar Rydzinski—thank you for always going to bat for all the things I write.

To my editor, Mary Kate Castellani, for her humor, her warmth, and her excellent editorial notes; and to the team at Bloomsbury: Diane Aronson, Erica Barmash, Sean Curran, Beth Eller, Courtney Griffin, Melissa Kavonic, Cindy Loh, Donna Mark, Lizzy Mason, Brittany Mitchell, Catherine Onder, Emily Ritter, and Claire Stetzer; to Patricia McHugh, for her careful read of the manuscript; and to Kim Smith, for yet another adorable cover that perfectly captures the members of TKC.

To Amy Bressler, Jennifer Daly, Regan Hofmann, Arielle Warshall Katz, Laura Liss, Geralyn Lucas, Sarah Mlynowski, Bianca Turetsky, and Meg Wolitzer, who answer the phone all hours of the day, whenever I need them.

To Sue Lawshe, for letting me pick her brain on all things quilting (anything that sounds like something a quilter would know is thanks to Sue; any mistakes are my own); and to Adele Griffin, Katie Hartman, and Kai Williams, my trusted readers (and re-readers), for their kind—and honest—notes.